World myths

Author: Coleman, Wim.
Reading Level: 5.1 MG
Point Value: 6.0
ACCELERATED READER QUIZ 2237

D1606184

Retold Myths & Folktales

African Myths

African American Folktales

Asian Myths

Classic Myths, Volume 1

Classic Myths, Volume 2

Classic Myths, Volume 3

Mexican American Folktales

Native American Myths

Northern European Myths

World Myths

The Retold Tales® Series features novels, short story anthologies, and collections of myths and folktales.

Perfection Learning®

Contributing Writers

Wim Coleman, Jr.
M.A.T. English and Education
Educational Writer

Pat Perrin
Ph.D. Art Theory and Criticism
Educational Writer

Retold Myths & Folktales

World Myths

Perfection Learning®

Editor in Chief
Kathleen Myers

Managing Editor
Beth Obermiller

Senior Editor
Marsha James

Editors
Terry Ofner
Christine LePorte

Cover Illustration
Mark Bischel

Inside Illustration
Sam Van Meter

Book Design
Dea Marks

For information contact
Perfection Learning® Corporation
1000 North Second Avenue, P.O. Box 500
Logan, Iowa 51546-0500
Phone: 1-800-831-4190 • Fax: 1-800-543-2745
perfectionlearning.com

PB ISBN-13: 978-1-5631-2209-5 ISBN-10: 1-5631-2209-x
RLB ISBN-13: 978-0-7807-1474-8 ISBN-10: 0-7807-1474-1

15 16 17 18 19 20 PP 13 12 11 10 09 08

T A B L E
O F   C O N T E N T S

WELCOME TO THE
RETOLD WORLD MYTHS

The world is full of variety. Every country—indeed, every locale—has it's own language, food, and view of the world. Another very special expression of this variety is mythology.

Myths tell a great deal about a culture. Such stories show how a people explained the mysteries of life and nature. Where did the stars come from? How did the human race spring into being? Why do people die? Myths provide fascinating answers to such questions.

Myths also express a culture's values. The story of a man's quest to save his people shows how heroism, strength, goodness, and wisdom are defined. And along with teaching values, myths teach lessons. For instance, a myth might demonstrate how dangerous it is to insult a stranger.

Finally, myths are simply great stories. Filled with drama, beauty, and even humor, they still attract listeners thousands of years after they were first told.

RETOLD UPDATE

This book presents a collection of eight adapted myths from around the world. All the variety, excitement, and humorous details of the original versions are here. But in the *Retold* versions of the stories, long sentences and paragraphs have been split up.

In addition, a word list has been added at the beginning of each story. Each word defined on that list is printed in dark type within the story. If you forget the meaning of one of these words, just check the list to review the definition.

You'll also find footnotes at the bottom of some story pages. These notes identify people or places, explain ideas, show pronunciations, or provide cultural information.

We offer two other features you may wish to use. One is a map of the world on the following page. This map locates the region where each of the myths were first told.

You will find more cultural information in the Insights sections after each myth. These revealing and sometimes amusing facts will give you insights into the ancient cultures, the tellers of the myths, or related myths.

One last word. Since many of these myths have been retold often, many versions exist. So a story you read here may differ from a version you read elsewhere.

Now on to the myths. Remember, when you read the *Retold World Myths,* you bring each story back to life. We hope you'll discover the beauty and excitement of these stories from around the world.

WORLD MAP

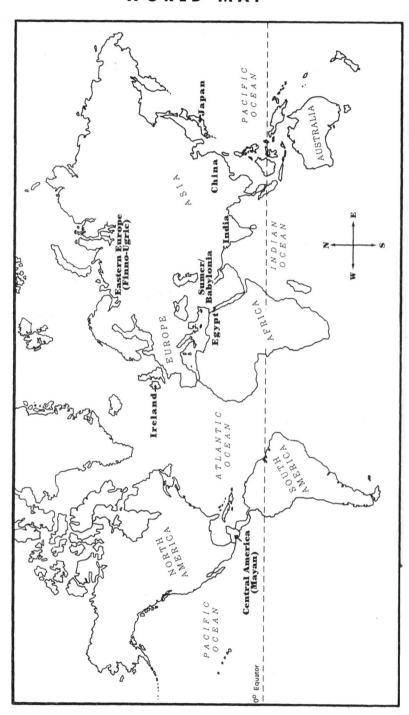

THE DEATH OF OSIRIS

VOCABULARY PREVIEW

Below is a list of words that appear in the story. Read the list and get to know the words before you read the story.

appease—calm; lessen
barren—lifeless
brooding—thinking seriously
contended—claimed; stated
craned—stretched
cunning—sly; clever
descended—moved downward
drastic—extreme
eternity—endless time; life after death
exquisite—beautifully made
fertile—able to produce life
former—previous; earlier
frenzied—wild; out of control
immortal—able to live forever
intact—in one piece
intrigued—fascinated; charmed
labored—heavy; difficult
resented—took offense at; felt anger at
sorely—painfully; unbearably
wailing—crying loudly

Main Characters

Horus—son of Isis and Osiris
Isis—wife of Osiris
Nephthys—Set's wife
Osiris—pharaoh of Egypt; husband of Isis and father of Horus
Set—brother to Osiris

The
Death of *Osiris*

A myth from Egypt

The kingdom of Egypt
is wisely ruled by the powerful
gods Osiris and Isis.
But even the gods aren't safe from
the jealous schemes of others.
Osiris' evil brother, Set, wants the throne
for himself. And he's figured out a
way to get it—by offering his
brother a special "gift."

*O*siris[1] closed his eyes and sighed wearily. Would the party never end? All this drinking and laughing and joking was giving him a headache. He was ready to go home.

Osiris looked around him. No one else acted like they were ready to leave. He sighed again. "I'll stay just a few more minutes," he said to himself. "Then I'll go home to my wife. I don't care if I *am* the guest of honor."

Osiris was Egypt's pharaoh.[2] But he was no ordinary king—he was also a god. He was the great-grandson of Ra, the god who had created the earth.

---

[1] (ō sēr´ us)
[2] (fā´ rō) Pharaoh was the title of the ancient Egyptian kings.

Osiris was at his own homecoming party. The celebration had been planned by his brother Set.

Osiris and Set had never been particularly fond of each other. Osiris ruled the **fertile** land of Egypt with his wife Isis.[3] Set had to settle for governing the desert lands. For this reason, Set **resented** his brother's greater power.

So Osiris was surprised when Set invited him to the party. But Osiris wanted to trust his brother, so he accepted the invitation.

For the last several months, Osiris had been busy traveling throughout the land teaching the people how to grow food. He enjoyed his travels. But he was happy to be home again.

The pharaoh was especially glad to be back with his wife Isis. The lovely goddess had ruled the kingdom in her husband's absence. She had done a fine job.

Another loud burst of laughter from the party goers interrupted Osiris' thoughts.

"All right," Osiris thought. "I've had enough."

But just as he started to get up, he heard the voice of his brother Set.

"Quiet, everyone, I have something to say," Set announced.

Osiris sat back down. He would listen to whatever his brother had to say and then say good night.

"I have a surprise for you all," Set continued. "Something I hope you'll enjoy." Set then turned to face one of the doorways.

Osiris turned his gaze too. What he saw caused him to sit up. Several servants were carrying an empty casket[4] into the hall.

But this wasn't just any casket. It was the most beautiful one Osiris had ever seen.

A gasp of admiration followed the casket as it was brought to the front of the room.

"What do you think of it?" Set asked the crowd. "It was

---

[3] (ī´ sis)

[4] A casket is a box used for burial. The Egyptians buried their dead in beautifully carved coffins that were built to fit the dead person.

made especially for this dinner by the finest carpenters in the land."

Osiris and the other guests **craned** their necks to get a closer look. The lid and sides of the casket were decorated with **exquisite** designs. And the entire box was covered with gold and jewels.

The Egyptians took great delight in such a well-made casket. They knew that earthly life was but a step toward the next. One's burial place needed to be pleasant in order to enjoy a happy life in the world to come. That's why the Egyptians built large tombs and furnished them well.

The dinner guests could see that this casket was special. Every one of them would be happy to spend **eternity** in such a charming place.

"We're going to have a contest," Set announced. "Everyone shall try out the coffin. The lovely casket shall belong to the person who fits it perfectly."

Immediately everyone scrambled to the front of the dining hall. Each wanted to be the first to lie down in the casket.

Osiris stayed behind and watched. He forgot about wanting to go home.

"How wonderful it would be to have such a casket for myself," he thought. "But is it proper for someone of my rank to take part in such a game? After all, I am pharaoh."

As Osiris looked on, the guests tried out the casket one by one. However, no one seemed to be an exact fit. They were either too short or too tall. Or they were too fat or too thin.

At last everyone except Osiris had lain in the coffin. And everyone except Osiris wore a disappointed look.

Set looked at his brother. "You must try it, Osiris," he declared.

The pharaoh was doubtful at first. "I'm not sure I should do this," he said.

But the guests encouraged him.

"None of us fit, Osiris," one said. "You're the only one left."

Osiris walked up to the casket and looked in. It certainly seemed to be close to his size. What would be the harm in just trying it out?

Without delay, Osiris climbed into the coffin and lay down.

"A perfect fit!" cried one of the guests.

"The casket is yours!" exclaimed another.

Set walked over to the casket and peered inside.

"Yes," he said, smiling down at his brother. "Just as I planned." His smile suddenly grew cruel. "Dear brother. You're going to the Underworld earlier than expected."

Set's voice began to grow louder. "At last, this is my hour, Osiris."

"What are you talking about?" asked Osiris with a nervous laugh.

"*I* should have been named the ruler of all of Egypt. But your **cunning** wife Isis tricked our great-grandfather. She discovered his secret name and used it to gain power for you both.

"In the meantime," Set continued with anger in his voice, "I was left to rule the desert. What can I do with that?

"Nothing," Set answered himself. "Nothing grows there; few people live there. I feel like I rule a pile of sand.

"All that's going to change," Set **contended,** raising his voice. "Now *I* will rule all of Egypt. And you, Osiris, won't be around to stop me!"

With those words, Set slammed the lid of the coffin shut.

"Let me out!" Osiris called. "Set, there is no reason for this!"

From inside the dark casket, the trapped pharaoh heard nails being driven into the lid. Osiris began to panic as he realized that Set was trying to kill him!

Osiris' breathing grew more and more **labored.** The air in the coffin was quickly running out.

"Oh, Isis," thought Osiris, thinking of his beautiful wife. "Little do you know that as you sleep, your husband, the father of your son, is being murdered!"

Osiris felt himself being moved. In another moment he was falling. Suddenly he felt a sharp bump and heard a splash.

"I'm in water," was Osiris' last thought. Then he closed

his eyes and lost all consciousness.

❖   ❖   ❖

The next morning Isis sleepily opened her eyes and looked at the pillow next to her.

She sat up quickly. Where was Osiris? Surely the party hadn't lasted all night? Her thoughts were interrupted by a **frenzied** knock at the bedroom door.

"Oh, Isis," cried a servant upon entering. "I have some horrible news. Set has killed Osiris!"

"What?" Isis screamed. "No, it can't be. Not Osiris! Tell me it's not true!"

Isis soon found out it *was* so. She listened in disbelief as her servant told of Osiris' murder. Then she tore through the palace, **wailing** with grief.

No one could comfort her. She had lost her husband and partner. Her son Horus had lost his father. But worse than death, her noble husband would go without burial.

"Where will my husband spend eternity?" she cried. "He should be buried in the finest tomb on earth! Instead, he's lost in the muddy waters of the Nile!

"I've got to find him," Isis finally decided. "I can't just forget about him."

If anyone could manage that task, it was Isis. She was a mighty sorceress,[5] with the power to perform great magic.

Isis began her quest by changing herself into an elderly woman. Then she set out to find her dead husband.

The grieving goddess first followed the Nile, hoping against hope to find the coffin washed up against the bank. But she found no sign of it anywhere.

Isis didn't give up, though. She vowed to herself that she wouldn't stop searching until she had found Osiris.

❖   ❖   ❖

What had become of the unlucky pharaoh whose own brother had plotted against him?

Poor Osiris had quickly drowned as water filled the casket. Then the river carried him and his golden box out into

[5] A sorceress is a female magician.

the Green Sea.[6] The casket washed up on the Phoenician shore near the city of Byblos.[7] There a tamarisk[8] tree quickly sprang up around it. Before long the rapidly growing tamarisk completely enclosed the coffin within its trunk.

This is how a tree became the tomb of the god of all growing things. Perhaps that is why the tamarisk quickly grew to be the largest of its kind.

One day the king and queen of Byblos saw the tree and were impressed with its tall, straight trunk.

"What a perfect addition to our new palace," the king exclaimed.

The queen agreed. "And smell the tree's lovely perfume. Its heavenly scent will fill all the rooms."

So the tamarisk, with the coffin hidden inside, was used as a ceiling support for the great hall of the new palace of Byblos.

Meanwhile Isis had arrived at the Green Sea. She followed the shore, questioning every traveler she met along the way. At last she approached Byblos. There she began to hear stories of a wonderful tamarisk tree supporting the great hall of the palace.

"The tree gives off the most wonderful perfume," said travelers coming from that direction. "There has never been a tree like it in this land."

As Isis neared the palace, she immediately recognized the perfume. It was the favorite scent of her beloved husband.

"Osiris' body must be trapped inside that tamarisk tree," she thought. "But how can I get to the coffin if the tree is used as a support? To suddenly remove the tree will bring the new palace to the ground. Even cutting the tree open to remove the coffin might cause the ceiling to fall."

Wearily Isis sat down to rest while she tried to figure out what to do. As it should happen, the handmaidens[9] of the queen of Byblos came by. Isis greeted them warmly.

---

[6] The Green Sea was the Egyptian name for the Mediterranean.

[7] Byblos was located near present-day Beirut, Lebanon.

[8] A tamarisk is a tree with tiny narrow leaves that grows in desert areas.

[9] Handmaidens are female servants.

The young women were **intrigued** by this strange woman who looked like one of royal blood. "She is clearly from a foreign country," said one handmaiden to another.

The handmaidens took Isis in, giving her a place to rest and food to eat. In turn, Isis quickly became a favorite of the young girls. She showed them new ways to arrange and perfume their hair. She secretly used her magic to help them with their daily problems.

After a short time the handmaidens told their queen of the wonderful woman. The queen was curious, so she sent for Isis.

"Certainly this stranger is Egyptian," the queen thought when she stared into the sad, kind eyes of Isis. Egyptians were known to have magic powers.

"You must stay and be nurse to my young son," the queen of Byblos said to Isis.

The goddess readily agreed. Now she had an excuse to stay at the palace while she thought of a way to rescue her dead husband.

Isis soon grew to love the royal child. He reminded her of her own young son Horus, whom she **sorely** missed. She loved the baby so much that she decided to make him **immortal.**

Every night, she placed the baby on the burning coals of the fireplace. The spells she cast kept the baby from burning. "Don't be afraid, my child," the goddess cooed. "Soon you will be just like the gods."

But Isis' spells were interrupted one night when the child's mother entered the room unexpectedly.

The poor woman saw her baby in the fire and screamed in terror. "How dare you try to kill my baby!" she cried. "I trusted you!"

The king heard his wife's cries and rushed into the room. "What is the meaning of this?" he angrily demanded.

Isis was sad that the spell had been broken. Now the precious baby could never become immortal.

But then the goddess saw how frightened the child's parents were. To **appease** their fear, she removed her disguise.

There she stood in her full glory before the king and queen of Byblos.

The royal pair were awestruck. They knew at once that they faced a goddess—and that their son had received very special care indeed.

"Please forgive us, goddess. You must stay with us here in the palace," they invited.

"Thank you for your kind offer," Isis replied. "But I have found what I came for." She led them to the great hall and pointed to the tamarisk tree. "This noble tree is the tomb of my husband, the pharaoh Osiris. I didn't wish to destroy your palace by opening it."

The king and queen of Byblos were amazed. They now understood why the tamarisk was unlike any other tree in their kingdom. Quickly they called together the craftsmen who had built the palace.

"Tell us how to remove this tree," the king said to the builders. The head craftsman looked up at the ceiling and scratched his head. He studied how the tree supported the roof. He knew another tree like this was not to be found in the whole kingdom.

"Perhaps we can replace the tree with a support made of smaller trees," the craftsman said at last. "But we must build a structure to hold everything in place while we remove the tamarisk."

"Do it, then," commanded the King.

The structure was built, just as the craftsman had suggested. When that was done, the workers safely removed the tamarisk from the great hall. Then the king and queen of Byblos happily presented the tree to Isis.

"At last!" the goddess exclaimed. "At last I will be able to see my beloved husband again."

Isis used her magic to open the tree trunk, revealing the wonderful coffin. Then she opened the coffin and looked upon her husband's face.

The pharaoh was truly dead, but he looked as young and handsome as he had in life. The goddess flung herself across the coffin, weeping bitterly.

"Is there anything we can do to help?" the queen of Byblos offered in sympathy.

"No," Isis replied tearfully. "There is nothing anyone can do."

"At least let us provide you with a ship for your return home," the king insisted.

"Thank you," Isis said. "That is very kind."

As the ship carried her home, Isis silently sat beside the coffin. She was too wrapped up in her sorrow to move or speak.

The ship reached the Nile and began to make its way up the mighty river. Isis now saw that Egypt's very soil was no longer fertile. All green growth had turned brown. Egypt was beginning to look like the deserts of Set's **former** kingdom.

"How sad that Egypt suffers just as I do!" Isis thought. "Will the land itself die of grief over Osiris?"

Isis ran her hand over the designs carved into the coffin. "Dear Osiris," she whispered to her husband's body. "I brought you back to Egypt so that I could bury you—so that you would have a good afterlife. But Egypt suffers under Set's rule.

"We'll have to do something more **drastic,**" Isis continued. "I know of certain magical herbs[10] growing in the marshes. I shall use them and return you to life. But I must keep you hidden from Set. If he discovers what I mean to do, he'll ruin everything."

Isis ordered the ship's captain to land near the marshes along the river's edge. She carefully hid the casket among the reeds. Then she covered it with leaves and branches.

Isis walked far up the river bank, searching for the magical herbs. She didn't notice a pair of eyes poking out of the water, watching every move she made.

The eyes were those of a scaly crocodile who grinned wickedly as Isis searched the marsh. Unfortunately, the beast was one of Set's spies. Once the crocodile saw what Isis had done, he slipped beneath the surface without making a splash.

---

[10] Herbs are plants that are sometimes used as medicine or seasoning.

Swiftly the crocodile swam toward Set's new palace. In a short time, he was leading Set himself to the coffin.

"So Isis has found you," Set said to Osiris' body. "Perhaps she plans to bury you. Or maybe she would like to bring you back to life.

"Well, we can't have that!" said Set with a chuckle. "I know just what to do!"

Set knew how important it was for the body to remain **intact** after death. Otherwise, the soul itself would not live on into the next life. So Set pulled his brother's body from the coffin and chopped it into sixteen pieces. Then he scattered the pieces of the body far and wide across the land of Egypt.

"There!" he said, when his business was completed. "That will take care of Osiris—in this world and the next!" Sure of his success, Set returned to his palace.

When Isis had found the herbs she needed, she returned to where she had hidden the coffin. She froze in horror at what she saw.

The lid of the coffin was flung open. The casket was empty. A scrap of Osiris' royal robe floated in the water. Isis trembled, realizing at once what the wicked Set had done.

"You will not win this way, Set!" Isis screamed into the wind. Her tears flowed into the Nile. Every creature grieved with her. Even the crocodile felt ashamed of Set's awful deed.

Isis searched the marsh nearby. A few pieces of Osiris' body were scattered there. But many more remained unfound.

"I will find them if I have to search all of Egypt!" Isis declared. She hurried back to her palace and began to prepare for the long journey ahead.

Before she left, Isis was surprised to receive a visit from Set's wife, the goddess Nephthys.[11]

"Isis, my husband must be stopped," Nephthys said. "Set killed Osiris because he hates all good and is only capable of evil. If he remains pharaoh, all Egypt will become a desert. The world will be full of suffering forever."

Isis looked deep into her sister's eyes, wondering for a

[11] (nef′this)

moment if this might be a trick. But Isis knew that Nephthys was a friend of the dead. She would never mistreat a soul that had recently died.

"Come, then, and help me search," said Isis gratefully. "It will not be an easy task, and I welcome your help."

So Isis and Nephthys set out through the land of Egypt. They wandered far and near, patiently gathering the pieces of Osiris' body.

Everywhere Isis and Nephthys went, they saw crops failing and people starving. "We must hurry," Nephthys said to Isis. "Otherwise Set will rule the whole world."

Wherever Isis and Nephthys found one of the pieces of the body, the local people celebrated and built a temple to Osiris. Isis hoped she could help these kind people by restoring Osiris' life—and the life of the land.

At last, Isis and Nephthys returned to the palace of Egypt with all sixteen pieces. Isis carefully put the body of Osiris back together again. She rubbed her husband's dead limbs with oils and the herbal potion she had made. Slowly but surely, the pieces of the body grew back together.

Isis prayed over the body, calling upon friendly gods. Even her son Horus helped her. The powers of the gods and the effects of the herbs, oils, and potion all began to do their work. But the most powerful medicine was Isis' love for her husband.

Hour after hour Isis prayed. And hour after hour the air crackled and the earth trembled. At last everything grew silent, as though the world was holding its breath.

The next sound was a sigh from Osiris' lips. He opened his eyes and found himself staring at his wife. "Isis, my love," he breathed.

The goddess was overjoyed. "Osiris!" she cried as she embraced him. "How wonderful to have you back at last!"

Indeed, all Egypt was thrilled to have the pharaoh back. And it wasn't just the people who rejoiced. The moment Osiris breathed again, the land also came back to life. The fields turned green, and trees again grew leaves.

❖   ❖   ❖

Even though Osiris was brought back to life, his brother Set
still ruled over Egypt. For this reason, Osiris, Isis, and their
son Horus went into hiding.

Osiris was delighted to see his son again. "Horus will
soon be a fine young man," he told Isis proudly. "One day he
will be pharaoh."

Even in hiding the family lived happily for several
months. But then, toward the end of the summer, Isis noticed
that Osiris seemed less joyful. He looked tired and he spent
more and more time **brooding** by himself. Soon he seemed no
more than a shadow.

"Husband, something troubles you," said Isis with
concern. "Please tell me what it is."

Osiris sighed. "I no longer feel at home among the
living," he said sadly.

"What do you mean?" asked Isis.

"When my body was closed up in Set's coffin, my soul
wandered through the Underworld,[12] restless and searching.
There I learned all the ways of the dead.

"And now I think I know the Underworld better than I do
my own kingdom," he continued. "I have given the living all
the gifts I can. I want to return to the Underworld and help the
dead."

"But you can't!" cried Isis, tears forming in her eyes. She
ran to her husband and held him tightly. "Think of how Egypt
will miss you—and how *I* will miss you!"

"I know, I know," said Osiris softly. "I'm deeply grateful.
I have you to thank for letting me see my kingdom and my
son again. But there's a time for death as well as life—even
for gods.

"You know this as well as I do," he continued. "We both
understand the land. We've seen how floods come and go.
And after the floods, we've waited while the grain grows rich
and golden. Then, after the harvest, we've watched the land

[12] The Underworld is the home of the dead.

grow brown and **barren** until it comes time for life again.

"Isis, you brought me back to life," Osiris said with a smile. "And when you did, the land was renewed. After I am gone, you will be reminded of me every spring—when the land becomes green again."

Isis bowed her head and thought over what her husband had said. Finally she sadly nodded her head in agreement. She knew it would be selfish to try to keep him among the living.

But one thing worried her. "Set still controls Egypt," she said to Osiris. "Without you here, how can your son and I protect ourselves?"

"Use your magic to protect Horus while he is a child," said Osiris. "That won't be for long. Soon he will be old enough to defeat Set. And even in the Underworld, I will be able to send my help."

These words comforted Isis. "Osiris, I will always love you. But I understand why you have to leave. And I know that one day I will join you. That's what will keep me going. So until then, farewell, my love!"

Isis remained strong as her husband **descended** into the Underworld. After all, she was watching one of the world's great mysteries—the magic circle of life and death. As a sorceress and goddess, Isis knew this magic very well.

In the Underworld, Osiris took his rightful place as king. There he greeted the newly arrived souls and taught them the ways of the afterlife. He ruled with fairness over the dead, just as he had over living men and women.

❖   ❖   ❖

Not long after Osiris left the earth, Isis called her son to her side. She explained to him that he would one day rule Egypt. But he would have to defeat Set to do so.

"You'll need special powers to overthrow Set," Isis said. "I'm going to give you a secret word that will give you the power you need to be pharaoh. The word is the secret name of your great-great-grandfather—Egypt's first pharaoh. You must guard this word carefully."

Then bending low, she said, "The name is..."

INSIGHTS

Osiris was first the Egyptian god of vegetation and later the god of the Underworld. He represented two of the most important concerns of the Egyptians—the growing of food and death.

In fact, the ancient Egyptians were almost obsessed with death. They believed that much of their earthly time should be spent preparing for their eternal afterlife.

The Egyptians thought that everything humans needed during life on earth was also needed in the afterlife. For this reason tombs were stocked with items ranging from furniture to jewelry to musical instruments.

In the Egyptian view, the Underworld was a dark, nightmarish place. It was said to be divided into twelve regions. The gate to each region was guarded by a fierce demon. The dead could only pass by if they knew the correct password.

To journey through these dreadful regions, the souls of the dead needed help. So a map of the Underworld was placed in the coffins of the dead to steer them on their road.

Texts of magic spells were also buried with the dead so they could deal with the demons of the Underworld. Other spells enabled a dead person to find food. In fact, lack of food in the Underworld was one of the Egyptians' biggest fears.

With all this help, the dead might at last reach the end of the twelve regions. There the soul would be placed before Osiris and judged.

You've probably heard the saying "light as a feather." The ancient Egyptians took this literally.

After the dead souls made it through the Underworld, they still had to be judged by Osiris. It was believed that a dead person's heart was placed on a scale which was set before the god. The heart was then weighed against a feather. If the heart was lighter than the feather, that meant the person had led a good life on earth. That person could look forward to an enjoyable afterlife.

But woe to the poor soul whose heart was heavier than the feather. This person was doomed to be eaten by an evil monster.

The four gods in this story—Osiris, Isis, Nephthys, and Set— were not only related by marriage. They were also brothers and sisters. But it was not that unusual in the myths for a god to marry a brother or sister.

The same held true for Egyptian rulers. The royal families of ancient Egypt allowed marriage between brothers and sisters.

Isis was generally a kind and thoughtful goddess. But when younger, she brutally used her magic to gain a powerful position.

Isis made her move when she noticed the sun god, Ra, growing old and weak. Ra, the first pharaoh, was Isis' great-grandfather.

In her desire for power, Isis came up with a plan to strip Ra of his rule. But in order to do this, she first had to find out his secret name.

Isis used her magic to poison Ra. As Ra lay squirming in pain, Isis promised to cure him—if he would reveal his secret name. Ra agreed, thus giving Isis power over him.

The belief in the importance of a person's name isn't limited to ancient cultures. Even today, many people have secret names which they guard carefully. Like Ra, they fear that misuse of their names may harm them.

Though Isis may have known the sun god's secret name, scholars today aren't sure what it was.

continued

Many ancient Egyptian myths were written down using hieroglyphics, a type of picture writing. Vowels weren't used in this type of writing, so we have to guess what they were. For instance, some scholars write "Re" to refer to the Egyptian sun god. Others spell his name "Ra."

As told in the myth, Horus was to follow Osiris as Egypt's ruler. But first he had to battle his uncle Set. Set was still determined to rule Egypt himself.

The day finally came when Horus and Set met in combat. According to one myth, Horus won the battle and took Set prisoner. But Isis took pity on Set, who after all was still her brother. She released him.

This enraged Horus. He chased after his mother and chopped off her head.

But the moon-god, Thoth, was keeping an eye on things. For some reason, he chose to rescue Isis by changing her head into a cow's head and attaching it to her body. That's why Isis is sometimes pictured wearing cow's horns.

Eventually, Horus did triumph over his uncle. He went on to rule Egypt, just as his parents had planned.

THE TWINS' VISIT TO THE UNDERWORLD

VOCABULARY PREVIEW

Below is a list of words that appear in the story. Read the list and get to know the words before you read the story.

agile—nimble; quick
appetizing—tasty; flavorful
avenge—take revenge on behalf of someone
commotion—disturbance; uproar
devised—designed; thought out
dismal—dreary; gloomy
emerged—came out
features—parts of the face
felines—cats
fiends—demons; monsters
leery—careful; on one's guard
misshapen—twisted; deformed
obligingly—willingly; agreeably
ravine—small, steep cut in the earth, usually made by running water
resurrected—brought back to life
scuttling—scampering; bustling
severed—cut off
shunned—avoided; scorned
soundly—completely
tremors—violent shaking; earthquakes

Main Characters

Hunahpú—"god of the hunt"; twin to Ixbalanqué
Ixbalanqué—his name means "little Jaguar"; twin to Hunahpú
Lords of Xibalba—rulers of the underworld

THE TWINS' VISIT TO THE UNDERWORLD

A Mayan myth from Central America

The Mayan twins have been challenged to a ball game by the lords of the underworld. To lose means death for the twins—and the lords have never been beaten. But playing ball is not all the twins have to worry about.

---

*R*unning at full speed, Hunahpú[1] skillfully bounced the rubber ball off his head. In return his twin brother, Ixbalanqué,[2] bounced the ball off his hip. Then the brothers rushed toward the goal—a stone hoop set in the wall above their heads.

[1] (hoon a poo´)
[2] (ish´ bal an kā´)

The twins were playing an exciting game of tlachtli.[3] But as exciting as their play was, it also brought back some sad memories for the twins.

"This is the same court that our father and uncle used to play on," noted Hunahpú. "That is, before they were defeated by the lords of Xibalba."[4]

"Yes," replied Ixbalanqué. "Perhaps if we play loud enough, we can wake the evil lords from their sleep."

With that, Ixbalanqué shot the ball straight through the hoop. The twins jumped up and down in excitement, for such shots were nearly impossible.

Indeed the two made such a **commotion** that the earth shook beneath their feet. Far below, the lords of the underworld felt the **tremors** and woke from their long sleep.

"Someone is playing tlachtli up there," said one of the lords.

"They're playing on the court right above us," replied another. "No one has played on that court since Hun-Hunahpú[5] and his twin brother years ago." Of course, the lord was referring to the twins' father and uncle.

"Judging from the noise they make," noted another, "we have a couple of new champions on our hands."

The lords of the underworld were great ball players themselves, and they hated to lose. So they decided to take action.

"We better not wait to challenge these new players to a game," said one of the lords. "They may get so good that they defeat us."

So the lords sent for one of their messengers—an old owl.

"We need you to go to earth," the lords told the owl. "Find these new ball players. If they're as good as they sound, invite them to visit us. Say that we've challenged them to a ball game here in Xibalba."

The owl left at once. He had no trouble finding the tlachtli

[3] (tlach´ tlē)
[4] (shi bal´ ba) Xibalba is the name of the Mayan Underworld. It is also the name of the underworld lords themselves.
[5] (hoon´ hoon a poo´)

champions. All he had to do was follow the tremors to their source.

The owl watched Ixbalanqué and Hunahpú play with admiration. It was soon clear that they were truly excellent players.

When the game was over, the owl went up to the twins and greeted them.

"You play well," said the owl.

The brothers thanked him, but they were not sure why an owl would be interested in tlachtli.

"I carry a message from the lords of Xibalba," the owl continued. "They wish to challenge you to a game."

Hunahpú and Ixbalanqué looked at one another.

"How do we know this isn't some kind of trick?" Hunahpú asked the owl.

"The lords heard you play, and they figured you must be pretty good," replied the owl. "They just want to find out. You know that tlachtli is their favorite game, don't you?"

"Yes, and they're good," said Ixbalanqué. "The lords of Xibalba defeated our father and uncle."

The two young men were silent for a moment. They both thought of their father, Hun-Hunahpú, who had also been a tlachtli champion.

"Our father and uncle never returned from that game," remarked Hunahpú.

"That is so," replied the owl. "They lost. So the lords of Xibalba cut off their heads and hung them from a calabash[6] tree."

"If we accept this challenge, we could lose our heads," said Ixbalanqué.

"Perhaps," Hunahpú replied. "But we both know that we're better players than our father and uncle. There's a strong chance that we're good enough to defeat the Xibalba."

"It would also give us a chance to **avenge** the deaths of our father and uncle," said Ixbalanqué.

"Tell the lords of the underworld that we accept their

---

[6] A calabash is a tropical American fruit tree.

challenge," said Hunahpú to the owl.

As soon as the owl left, the twins started preparing for their trip. They packed special tlachtli gear—arm and hip guards made of rubber and colorful ankle bracelets. They also packed several of their own rubber tlachtli balls.

In a short time, Ixbalanqué and Hunahpú were heading down the long black road to the underworld. They crossed a deep **ravine** with a boiling hot river steaming below. Then they crossed another river that flowed with blood. On and on they followed the black road. Finally they came to a gate in a stone wall.

"This must be Xibalba," said Ixbalanqué. "Sure does seem gloomy."

Suddenly Hunahpú gasped. "Look over there!" he exclaimed, pointing at a calabash tree. From it hung two heads.

"Father! And uncle!" Ixbalanqué said in a hushed voice.

"With luck, our heads won't end up beside theirs," added Hunahpú.

As the twins stared at the tree, the lords of Xibalba walked up to meet them.

"Greetings," said the lords to the twins. "And welcome to Xibalba. We are delighted you've accepted our challenge."

Hunahpú and Ixbalanqué studied the lords, carefully sizing them up. The Xibalba seemed kindly enough at first glance, but the twins were **leery.** They knew that before long, they would be playing those lords in a game of life and death.

"Please make yourselves at home in one of our fine guest houses," said one of the lords with a little smile. "We'll play ball first thing in the morning."

Ixbalanqué and Hunahpú were then led to a stone building called the House of Gloom. The structure certainly lived up to its name. The inside was totally dark. There wasn't a single window to let in a glimmer of light.

"Fine hosts we have," grumbled Ixbalanqué.

"I'll say," agreed Hunahpú. A sudden noise caught his attention.

"Listen," he said. "Do you hear strange **scuttling** noises? I bet they've sent demons to frighten us."

"Let's not light our torches," suggested Ixbalanqué. "We don't want to attract these monsters."

The twins felt around in the dark, trying to find a bed—or at least a few comfortable chairs. But there seemed to be no furniture at all.

Muttering under their breath, the two settled down on the cold, rough floor.

The twins survived that dark and frightening night in the House of Gloom. But they didn't get much sleep. All night long the unseen demons filled the air with unearthly howls and screams. Ixbalanqué and Hunahpú were constantly on guard, afraid of being attacked in the dark.

Nevertheless, when morning came, Hunahpú and Ixbalanqué boldly marched out to the ball court. And they **soundly** defeated the lords of the underworld! In fact, the twins were so skillful at passing the ball back and forth that the Xibalba never really gained control of the ball at all.

The lords were furious. No one had ever beaten them before.

"We can't let them get away with this," declared one lord. He called the twins over.

"You must give us a gift," the lord said to them.

"Tomorrow you must bring us four bunches of flowers," said another lord. "You must hand them over before our next game begins."

Hunahpú and Ixbalanqué looked at each other in puzzlement. They had just won the tlachtli game. So why should they bring the lords a gift? And besides, where would they find flowers in the underworld?

But the twins didn't dare protest, for the lords were too powerful. So they politely agreed.

With that, the lords led Hunahpú and Ixbalanqué to their second guest house—the House of Knives. This place would prove to be even worse than the House of Gloom.

As they entered, the twins realized that the house was a dark prison. "How are we supposed to find flowers in this **dismal** place?" asked Ixbalanqué.

Before Hunahpú could respond, they both heard something move. What the twins saw next made them both forget about flowers. Before them stood a group of monstrous **fiends** holding spears.

"We're trapped!" said Ixbalanqué in a whisper. "What can we do? We have no weapons."

"I don't know. But we'd better act fast," warned Hunahpú. "Our hosts don't look very friendly."

At that moment, one of the fiends pointed his razor-sharp spear at Hunahpú's face. Another fiend aimed his spear at Ixbalanqué. Behind those two monsters stood many more, all armed in the same way.

Ixbalanqué thought quickly. "You look like a hungry fellow," he said to the fiend standing in front of him. "Too bad you don't have anything better than my brother and me to eat."

"Yes, too bad," agreed Hunahpú. "We won't be tasty at all. I'll bet you'd rather have some nice animal meat."

The fiends exchanged glances and slowly nodded. The twins really didn't look very **appetizing.**

"Kill us if you like," said Hunahpú pleasantly. "But maybe we can make some kind of deal."

"That's right," continued Ixbalanqué. "Once we get out of here, we promise to return with lots of meat."

The fiends lowered their spears and stared stupidly at the twins. Their mouths watered at the very idea of animal meat. They grumbled a little among themselves, then wandered off into different parts of the house.

Hunahpú and Ixbalanqué breathed deep sighs of relief. They were safe—at least for that night. In fact, the only sensible thing to do was sleep. So the twins looked around for a bed. But they couldn't spot one in that gloomy place. Finally they chose a corner and settled down for another night's sleep on the floor.

But Hunahpú couldn't put the coming day out of his mind. He kept wondering what would happen when they showed up on the court with no flowers.

Hunahpú rolled over on his side and gazed into the dark

room. Suddenly he gave a little jump. A line of ants was marching past his face. Hunahpú sat up carefully, so as to not crush any of the insects. He reached out and touched his brother's shoulder.

Ixbalanqué hadn't been sleeping either. His eyes widened when he saw the parade. Ixbalanqué leaned over and spoke softly to the ants. Hunahpú did likewise. Following a long, quiet conversation, the ants promised to help the twins. After that, Hunahpú and Ixbalanqué finally went to sleep.

When the twins woke early the next morning, they saw that the ants had kept their promise. A steady stream of fresh flowers moved across the floor toward the twins. Each flower was carried by several ants.

The ants put the flowers in a pile between Hunahpú and Ixbalanqué. When there were enough flowers for four bunches, the twins thanked the ants politely.

Before long the lords of the underworld arrived at the House of Knives and unlocked the door. They were amazed to see the twins still very much alive. They were even more astounded when Ixbalanqué and Hunahpú each held out two bunches of fresh flowers.

The lords accepted the flowers as calmly as they could. But they were so upset that they lost the tlachtli game again that day.

From then on, the twins' visit to the underworld settled into a kind of routine. Each morning Hunahpú and Ixbalanqué played ball against the lords of the Xibalba. Sometimes the twins won and sometimes the game was a tie. But the lords of the underworld could never beat them. Then each night the twins were forced to stay in a different and more dangerous place.

One night the twins were sent to the House of Cold. Most people who slept there froze to death in their sleep.

"We must survive this somehow," Hunahpú said, his teeth chattering. "Remember what our grandmother told us when we were small?"

"Yes," replied Ixbalanqué, shivering. "There are six houses here in Xibalba. Anyone who can survive a night in each one becomes immortal."

"If we don't find a way to get warm soon, this will be the last house we see," said Hunahpú.

Ixbalanqué and Hunahpú searched the barren house. Just when they thought they couldn't stand it anymore, they found some old logs and knots from pine trees. Quickly the twins built a fire and huddled together for warmth. So they survived the House of Cold.

Another night, Hunahpú and Ixbalanqué were sent to the House of Jaguars.[7] There they were surrounded by hungry **felines,** who growled and spit and clawed at them. But the twins found some old bones and threw them to the beasts. The jungle cats were satisfied, and the twins **emerged** unhurt the next morning.

Hunahpú and Ixbalanqué also survived the House of Fire by dodging all around its dancing flames. The twins didn't sleep at all that night. Still, they managed to tie the lords in their tlachtli game the following day.

But the twins spent the most horrible night of all in the House of Bats. As soon as they entered, giant mouselike creatures swooped down upon them. These bats had long dangerous teeth and wing tips as sharp as spears.

"This looks like our last evening in Xibalba," said Ixbalanqué. "I can't see how we can possibly survive the night in a place like this."

Then Hunahpú noticed something. "Look," he hurriedly said to his brother. "The bats never seem to touch the floor. Let's try lying flat on the ground. Then maybe we'll be safe from their sharp teeth and wing tips."

Without further delay, the brothers flung themselves down. And Hunahpú's plan seemed to work. As the night wore on, Ixbalanqué and Hunahpú started to think they might survive after all.

But then Hunahpú made a terrible mistake—he raised his head to see what the bats were doing. With a hideous shriek,

---

[7] A jaguar is a tropical American wildcat. It is brownish-yellow with black spots and is larger than a leopard.

the Lord of the Bats dove at Hunahpú and sliced off his head.

Poor Ixbalanqué could do nothing to help his brother. He feared the same would happen to him if he moved even a finger.

The next morning the lords of Xibalba unlocked the door to the House of Bats. Of course, they were expecting to find both twins dead. To their delight, the first thing they saw was Hunahpú's **severed** head.

"But where's the other brother?" asked one of the lords. "If he were dead, surely his head would lie here as well."

"It doesn't matter if he's dead or not," said another lord. "If he meets us on the playing field alone this morning, he doesn't stand a chance of winning."

Laughing noisily, the lords of the underworld took Hunahpú's head to the ball court. There they hung it up as a trophy.

As for Ixbalanqué, he wasn't dead. He was hiding in another part of the house. And although Hunahpú was headless, he wasn't dead either. Of course, without his head he couldn't see or hear or smell or speak. But his body could still stand and walk.

The House of Bats had been the sixth and last house. Ixbalanqué knew he had won immortality by surviving it. But the thought didn't cheer him.

"Unless I find a way to get my brother's head back soon, he'll die," thought Ixbalanqué.

Ixbalanqué sadly led his brother's headless body out of the House of Bats. Where in this cruel place could he find help? He knew better than to ask for aid from the Xibalba.

Then Ixbalanqué remembered how the ants helped them find flowers. "Perhaps the animals will help me," he thought.

So Ixbalanqué called all the animals of the underworld together in a meadow. Swift rabbit, strong-winged hawk, and **agile** goat—at least one of every kind of animal—gathered around the brothers. The last to appear was the turtle, who crawled slowly up behind the rest.

"Friends, I need your help," said Ixbalanqué. "My brother, Hunahpú, has been injured in the House of Bats. The wound is pretty serious, as you can see. His body still lives, but his strength is failing. I'm afraid the lords of the underworld will destroy us both—as they destroyed our father and our uncle."

At this the animals chattered and squealed and snorted and barked. One rabbit remarked, "I'd like to help you, but I can't think what to do."

In fact, none of the noisy animals could think of a way to help the twins. One by one, they fell silent.

Finally the silent turtle walked forward. Ixbalanqué looked at the little animal and was filled with despair. What could a turtle possibly do to help?

By this time, Hunahpú's body was slumped on the ground. Without a word, the turtle crawled to the body and climbed up onto Hunahpú's shoulders.

When the turtle reached Hunahpú's neck, he stuck fast. Then the turtle roughly took the shape of the head. Suddenly Hunahpú sat up straighter.

Ixbalanqué rushed to his brother. He could see that Hunahpú was growing stronger again.

"Brother," said Ixbalanqué, "sit still and I'll shape your **features.**"

Rapidly Ixbalanqué pushed and pulled at the tough, turtle-shell head. First, he shaped a nose that looked like Hunahpú's. He was relieved to see the nose drawing deep breaths of air. Then Ixbalanqué formed ears that looked like Hunahpú's.

"Brother, can you hear me?" Ixbalanqué asked.

Hunahpú nodded with his strange new head. Feeling encouraged, Ixbalanqué pushed and pulled until he had made two eyes that looked liked Hunahpú's. The eyes blinked at him and gazed around the meadow.

Finally Ixbalanqué shaped a mouth similar to Hunahpú's. Now Hunahpú could speak.

"My thanks to you, brother," said Hunahpú with his new mouth. "And thanks to the noble turtle who has loaned himself to me. Now I can see and hear and smell and speak. But if I'm to be in top form for the game today, we must figure out how to get my own head back."

The brothers whispered together and worked out a plan

for defeating the Xibalba in the tlachtli game. They called the rabbit who had said he wanted to help. Quietly they shared their plan with him.

"I can help! I can help!" squealed the rabbit, jumping up and down with excitement.

The rabbit ran off into the tall grass, and the twins went to the ball court. Of course, the Xibalba were astonished to see the brothers appear, looking ready for a good game of tlachtli.

The lords turned and stared at Hunahpú's head, still hanging in the ball court. Then they turned back to look at the new head on Hunahpú's body. The new head looked like Hunahpú, all right. But there was still something wrong with it. It was rough and **misshapen,** like an unfinished sculpture.

"This is surely some kind of trick," said one of the lords.

"Well, it's not likely to work," said another.

The lords of the Xibalba laughed and took their places on the tlachtli court. They were sure that a man with a weird head could never beat them at their favorite ball game.

But Ixbalanqué and Hunahpú knew exactly what they were doing. On the very first play, Ixbalanqué hit the ball far out of the court into the tall grass. The rabbit, who had been hiding there, jumped up and chased after the ball.

"That rabbit will get our tlachtli ball!" screeched one of the lords of the underworld.

"Quick, chase the rabbit away!" yelled another lord. "Someone get the ball!"

All the Xibalba ran after the rabbit. Ixbalanqué took advantage of that moment of confusion. He leapt up and snatched Hunahpú's real head from where it hung over the tlachtli court.

Seeing that he was no longer needed, the turtle freed itself from Hunahpú's neck. Quickly, Ixbalanqué put his brother's real head back in place. Then the twins gently lowered the turtle to the ground and thanked him for his help.

As the turtle waddled off the court, Hunahpú's features faded from his shell. By the time he disappeared into the tall grass, he looked like a normal turtle again.

When the Xibalba returned to the court with the ball, they

were amazed to see that Hunahpú had his own head back. But there was nothing the lords could do except continue the game—and lose. With both of them back in action, the brothers easily won.

After the game, the Xibalba team got together to discuss their situation.

"We're never going to beat these twins in a tlachtli match," said one of the lords.

"We'll have to finish them off some other way," said another.

"But how? They've survived six nights in our terrible houses. What else can we do?"

The lords of Xibalba talked and argued for a long time. Finally they **devised** a plan. They built a huge bonfire near the ball court. Then they invited Hunahpú and Ixbalanqué to join them.

"We have another game we like to play," one of the lords said to the twins. "We take turns running through the flames."

"Will you join us at our game?" asked another.

The twins glanced at one another. They knew that the lords of the underworld were up to no good. But after their adventure in the House of Fire, one bonfire didn't look too frightening.

"We'll be happy to join you at your game," said Hunahpú.

"Then be our guest," said one of the lords. "Please go first."

The twins both laughed, then leapt willingly into the flames. Within moments, their bodies were burned to ashes.

Of course, the lords of Xibalba didn't enter the flames at all. Cheering and celebrating their trick, they took the twins' ashes to the Sea of Xibalba. And there they scattered the ashes with cruel laughter.

However, the twins had known exactly what they were doing. Since their brave deeds had earned them immortality, no fire could ever kill them.

Five days later, Hunahpú and Ixbalanqué were **resurrected.** In the shapes of poor fishermen, they appeared among the lords. The brothers looked ragged and dirty. But because they danced and entertained the lords of the underworld, they were welcomed.

Some of their best tricks had to do with fire. They burned down buildings and magically restored them. Then they took turns burning each other. Even though nothing remained of their bodies except ashes, the twins sprang back to life unharmed. They even burned a dog and brought it back to life.

The lords of the underworld were amazed at the twins' magic. When they saw living things killed and restored to life again and again, they wanted to share the experience. So the Xibalba asked the fishermen to perform the magic on them.

At first the fishermen refused.

"Oh, no," said Hunahpú shyly. "We're just two ragged fishermen, and this is just a simple trick."

"We don't deserve to have fine lords like you honor us by taking part," added Ixbalanqué.

These words made the lords of the underworld even more determined. They loudly insisted on taking part in this wonderful magic.

Finally the sly fishermen agreed. Ixbalanqué and Hunahpú **obligingly** burned the lords of the underworld. But there they stopped. They never brought the Xibalba leaders back to life.

When the people of the underworld saw that their lords were truly dead, they knew better than to fight the twins. They begged the brothers for mercy. Hunahpú and Ixbalanqué agreed not to kill them. But they did make certain rules.

"You people of the underworld shall be **shunned** by the people above," said Ixbalanqué.

"Your only food shall be the flesh of wild animals," said Hunahpú.

"And you shall no longer be allowed to play ball," said Ixbalanqué.

The people of the underworld groaned and protested—especially at the last rule. They loved to play ball more than anything. But the Xibalba had no choice but to accept their situation.

Before they left the underworld, the twins took the heads of their father and uncle down from the calabash. Then they returned to the surface of the earth, each carrying one of the heads.

When they reached the surface, the twins tossed the two heads into the air. The heads soared up into the sky. One became the sun and the other became the moon.

"Now we have truly avenged the deaths of our father and uncle," said Ixbalanqué.

"And we've proven we are the best ball players ever," added Hunahpú.

The brothers grinned at each other, pleased with their victory. Then they set off for the ball court, ready to play another game of tlachtli.

INSIGHTS

The story of the twins is one of the myths included in the Popol Vuh, the sacred book of the Maya.

The Popol Vuh is similar in a way to the Old Testament. It begins with a creation story. This story tells of the gods' several attempts to make a living thing that would worship them. The last part of the work is a history of the ancestors of the Maya, including both real and legendary people.

The Maya and other people who lived in Mexico and Central America actually played the ball game you read about in the myth. A similar game is still played today in parts of northern Mexico.

The tlachtli game was played on a long and narrow ball court measuring around 75 feet long and 25 feet wide. Low walls or benches marked the boundaries on each side.

The game itself roughly resembled a combination of basketball, volleyball, and soccer. Teams ranged in size from two to eleven men each.

The object of the game was to get a small but heavy rubber ball through rings or hoops placed at each end. The contest was made more difficult in that the ball could only be hit with the thighs, shoulders, heads, or arms—never the hands, feet, or lower legs.

It is thought that tlachtli had a religious significance. This is because the ball courts were usually built close to temples. No one is certain exactly what this significance was. But we do know that players often honored the sun god before a game.

The players on a Mayan ball team were very serious about winning. And well they should be. The captain of the losing team was often beheaded.

continued

The Maya were interested in more than just sports. They were also advanced astronomers. They had an amazing knowledge of the seasons and stars.

Using this knowledge, the Maya created a calendar that broke the year down into 20 months of 18 days each. Thus 20 x 18 made 360 days. Five extra calendar days were added at the end of the calendar to make a 365-day year. (By observing the skies, the Maya knew it took the earth 365 days to travel around the sun.)

The Maya were superstitious about the extra days. They felt that whatever they did during those five days they were doomed to do forever.

For that reason, the Maya were very careful during this time. For example, they tried not to get into a fight or trip while walking. Small wonder that many people elected to stay inside their houses until the five days were up.

The Maya had an interesting method of coping with a lack of rain. To get the attention of Chac—the god of rain—they burned balls of raw rubber. The thick smoke would rise up and form small stormlike clouds.

The people hoped that Chac would see the clouds and take his cue. If he did, the god would send some of his messengers to pour jars of water through the clouds.

The Maya didn't want too much rain, though. One of their most feared gods was the moon goddess Ixchel. She sent destructive floods down to earth when she became angry.

The Mayan pantheon (group of gods) is a large one. It more or less began with thirteen gods, one for each level of heaven. There were also nine lords who ruled the underworld, Xibalba. These lords were also gods, but they were constantly at war with the gods of heaven.

The Maya added new gods to the pantheon as the need for them arose. Most of the Mayan gods were nature gods such as the gods of the sun, moon, corn, etc. But there were also patron gods for just about every occupation—farmers, hunters, musicians, and dancers, to name a few.

In this myth, the twins burned a dog and brought it back to life. This magical deed had religious meaning for the Maya. In their culture, the dog was a symbol of death. In fact, it was customary to place a statue of a dog over a grave.

Just what lay beyond the grave? Another life, according to the Maya. Most of the dead went to paradise, where they spent their days relaxing under a large tree. But the truly evil were doomed to the dark underworld, where the cruel lords lay in wait for them.

The Mayan burial practices were similar to that of the Egyptians. Tombs were filled with objects people felt would be needed in the afterlife. And the rich or important people would need servants in the next life. So their tombs were also filled with bodies of sacrificed humans.

In addition, most tombs contained pottery and objects made of jade. These things were meant to be an offering to the gods—it was thought that the gods looked kindly on dead persons with such possessions.

FINN MacCOOL'S REVENGE

VOCABULARY PREVIEW

Below is a list of words that appear in the story. Read the list and get to know the words before you read the story.

abruptly—quickly; suddenly
agonized—worried
allegiance—loyalty
betrothed—one who is engaged to be married
conflicting—clashing; opposing
donned—put on
giddy—dizzy; light-headed
grimace—facial expression showing pain
hearth—floor in front of a fireplace
integrity—decency; honor
jilting—rejection
mourned—grieved
peril—danger
quarry—object of a hunt or chase
scowl—frown; look of displeasure
slay—kill
smolder—burn below the surface
truce—peace agreement
vaulted—leapt; jumped over
wavered—gave way; showed doubt

Main Characters

Angus—Diarmuid's foster father; magician
Diarmuid—member of the Fionna
Finn MacCool—leader of the Fionna; the most powerful warrior in the land; engaged to marry Grainne

Grainne—daughter of King Cormac; engaged to marry Finn
    MacCool
King Cormac—king of Ireland
Oisin—son of Finn; friend of Diarmuid

FINN MAC COOL'S REVENGE

A myth from Ireland

*Finn MacCool is one of the most highly
respected and powerful men in the land.
Yet he's soon to be betrayed by two of the people
dearest to him. Will he prove great enough to
overlook the insult? Or will he be betrayed
again—this time by his own temper?*

*O*n the day before her wedding was to take place,
Grainne[1] sat quietly among the noisy banquet guests. The
great hall of Tara, her father's castle, rang with laughter and
lively conversation. Warriors and ladies alike ate venison[2] and
brown bread and drank red wine.

"This great feast is being held for me," Grainne reminded
herself. "For me and my **betrothed.** This is the most
important banquet of my life." But the thought did not cheer
her up. Grainne did not feel like taking part in the merriment.

Grainne was a tall, bold girl with rich brown hair and rosy
skin. She was a very willful princess who was used to getting

---

[1] (grān´ nē)
[2] Venison is deer meat.

her way.

Tonight she sat to the left of her father, King Cormac. She watched the king as he raised his cup of wine in a toast.[3] Grainne loved her father and was proud of him. He was a noble man and a bold warrior. But now Grainne hardly heard what the king was saying.

She also watched her husband-to-be, the mighty warrior Finn MacCool. He was a large man with broad shoulders and a loud laugh. His eyebrows drew together toward the middle, giving his face a permanent **scowl.** Right now he was beaming with happiness.

Finn sat at the king's right hand. On Finn's other side were his Fionna[4] warriors, brave and noble men, every one. Finn raised his own goblet and said something in response to the words of the king.

"Now this is a fine man," Grainne told herself for the hundredth time. "You should be proud of such a match as this."

But as she watched Finn laugh and joke with his companions, Grainne did not feel proud. "I don't want to marry this man," she thought. "He's older than my father."

Grainne knew this shouldn't bother her. After all, it was not unusual for a young woman to be pledged to an older man.

But Grainne couldn't help the way she felt. "I still don't want to marry him," she thought again.

Finn's bravery was known throughout the land. His horses were swift and strong. He owned the best of the hunting hounds. Finn's men all followed him proudly. In addition, he had the power of healing. There was no reason why such a great hero should not have a new wife.

"But why does it have to be me?" Grainne wondered. No one had asked her. Grainne's father and Finn had made all the arrangements. Sometimes Grainne wished she weren't the daughter of the king. She let out a deep, sad sigh.

At the sound of Grainne's sigh, a nearby voice asked,

---

[3] A toast is a drink in honor of someone.
[4] (fē´ na) Fionna was the title of a group of fighting men in Ireland.

"Does something trouble you, my lady?"

Grainne started and blushed. She had barely noticed the warrior seated on her left. She was embarrassed that this stranger had noticed her sadness.

"No, of course not," Grainne snapped at the voice. She turned her head to see who had spoken.

She remembered his name now—Diarmuid.[5] She had first seen him earlier that day from a distance. Diarmuid was known as one of the Fionna's greatest fighters. The Fionna warriors always spoke highly of him. They liked to have the young warrior with them during battles or hunts. They said that Diarmuid was not only brave, but was noble of heart.

"This is a happy day for me," added Grainne, with an attempt at a smile. She looked the young warrior directly in the eyes.

Now it was young Diarmuid's turn to be embarrassed. He blushed slightly and looked down at his plate.

Grainne found such shyness very attractive. As she looked at Diarmuid, she realized that he was very handsome with his straight black hair and bright blue eyes.

As the banquet went on, the crowd at the table grew noisier. Grainne took advantage of the opportunity to find out more about the young warrior beside her. Diarmuid soon got over his shyness, and the two began chatting like old friends.

As they spoke the two felt themselves drawn to each other. They discovered that they were the same age and that they had much in common. Suddenly Grainne felt quite sure of what she wanted to do.

Whispering so that only Diarmuid would hear, Grainne said, "Noble warrior, I ask your help."

Diarmuid looked startled, but he was quick to reply. "Anything you wish, my lady Grainne, I will do. What beast do you wish me to **slay?** What kingdom you do you wish me to conquer for you?"

"I beg you to save me," said Grainne. "As you know, I am soon to marry Finn MacCool. I realize what a fine warrior he

[5] (dē ar´ mēd)

is—indeed, what a fine man he is. But I just can't bear the thought of being his wife." Grainne lowered her head sadly.

Diarmuid again looked embarrassed. Quietly he asked, "What is it you wish me to do?"

"Help me get away from this place," Grainne answered. "The wedding is tomorrow—a wedding I would rather miss."

Poor Diarmuid. What was he to do? It was obvious even to himself that he was falling in love with the young princess. But he was one of Finn's warriors. How could he betray his leader?

Grainne saw Diarmuid's discomfort. Gently she laid her hand on his. "I see that you are confused," she said. "But truly, Diarmuid, it is *you* that I want to marry. I speak so boldly because time is short. We have only this one night to set things right. And if we do not, I will spend the rest of my life in misery."

Diarmuid still hesitated. So Grainne took another step to bind the young warrior to her. Although she was young, she knew certain spells that were used by the druids.[6]

As the noise of the banquet roared over her head, Grainne leaned over and spoke the words of a spell into Diarmuid's ear. This spell created a bond between them—a bond that no one could break.

"Earlier you promised you would do anything to help me. I'm holding you to your word, noble warrior," said Grainne. "And now that promise is bound with magic. It is a warrior's oath, and you must keep it, Diarmuid."

Grainne knew that to pure and noble Diarmuid, such an oath would be unbreakable.

"You must take me away tonight," Grainne told Diarmuid. "I will see to it that everyone in the castle sleeps soundly. You must rescue me before morning. If you come after that, it will be too late. I will become Finn's wife, and you and I will never be together."

"My lady, you're asking a lot of me," Diarmuid said to Grainne. "I will need to think over this matter very carefully."

---

[6] (droo´ ids) Druids are priests of an ancient religion in the ancient British Isles.

The troubled warrior **abruptly** left the banquet.

Outside in the night air, Diarmuid looked up at the clear sky and the bright stars. All alone, he paced the wall of the castle and **agonized** over his problem.

Conflicting emotions burned within him. Diarmuid felt he had to do what Grainne wished. But he knew his head was clouded by feelings of love. And he knew as well that a true warrior would never betray his leader.

After a time Diarmuid saw one of the Fionna warriors approaching. It was his friend Oisin,[7] the son of Finn. Diarmuid decided to rely on the advice of his friend. He called Oisin to him and told him of his problem.

"Grainne has made me promise," he said as he ended his story. "And such a vow is not to be taken lightly. But I have also sworn **allegiance** to Finn."

Oisin looked thoughtful. Then he said, "Grainne would not have forced such a promise unless she were desperate. If she feels that strongly, she and my father would never be happy together. Better for Finn if you stop the wedding now."

"But is that really the right thing to do?" questioned Diarmuid.

"What do *you* want to do?" Oisin asked.

"With all my heart, I want to take Grainne away and make her my wife," said Diarmuid.

"Then follow your heart. However, you must beware of Finn for the rest of your life," Oisin warned. "He'll never forgive Grainne for not wanting him. And he may never forgive you for taking her away. I fear that you will have to face him someday."

With these words, Oisin left Diarmuid. But for a while longer, the honorable warrior paced back and forth. He continued to search his heart for the right action to take.

Meanwhile the banquet was winding down. But before the last of the wine was drained, Grainne sprinkled it with a magic potion. This potion was just strong enough to make sure those who drank it slept more soundly than usual. Then

[7] (oosh´ ēn)

she returned to her own room to wait for Diarmuid. The noise of the banquet gradually faded away.

Restlessly, Grainne paced back and forth. "Will Diarmuid rescue me?" she wondered. "Oh, I couldn't bear it if he's rejected me!" Grainne was close to tears.

Finally there was a slight sound at her door. Grainne threw the door open, and there stood Diarmuid. She flew into his arms. "Thank you, my love," she said, all her fears forgotten. "I knew you wouldn't let me down."

The two young people looked at each other, their hearts racing. Neither had ever been so in love before. They promised to be faithful to each other forever. Then they planned their escape from the castle.

Diarmuid and Grainne both held their breaths as they sneaked out through the castle. They tiptoed down long hallways past doorway after doorway. Everyone was sound asleep, including the guards. In the great hall, many of the guests slept right at the banquet tables. Even the hounds snored as they slept on the **hearth** in front of the dying fire.

"Walk very softly, my love," Grainne whispered. "We don't know for sure that all of the guards shared the drugged wine."

But they needn't have worried. No one woke to notice their departure. The couple lifted the bar on a small door in the castle wall and went out into the night.

Diarmuid had a chariot waiting just outside the castle walls. Grainne tossed her small bundle of food and clothing into the vehicle. Then she and Diarmuid set off.

Diarmuid drove until he came to the ford[8] of a wide river. But even at the ford, the water was too swift for the chariot to cross.

Diarmuid was determined that nothing would stop him. He bravely swept Grainne and her bundle up in his arms and carried her across the river. From there they were forced to continue their flight on foot. But they didn't mind. They were young and strong and **giddy** with their success.

[8] A ford is a shallow place suitable for crossing.

Soon the young couple came to a forest called the Wood of the Two Tents.[9] Here Diarmuid built a hut of small branches. Then the couple rested and ate some of the food Grainne had brought along.

"Finn will surely track us," Diarmuid said.

"Then we must keep moving," Grainne replied. "I am rested now. We must continue on our way as fast as we can go."

"No," said Diarmuid. "Sooner or later Finn will catch up with us. Someday I will have to face him. It might as well be here and now."

Diarmuid took his sword and began clearing trees from around the hut. Then he gathered the tree trunks and branches and began building a strong fence.

Back at the castle, all the guests slowly began to awake. As their fuzzy heads cleared, they continued with arrangements for the wedding. Someone went to wake and dress the bride, but she was not in her room.

"Search the castle," King Cormac ordered. "We can't have the bride late for her own wedding!"

But Grainne was nowhere to be found.

At first Finn and Cormac were bewildered. It had not occurred to them that Grainne might not want to be Finn's bride.

Then Cormac made a check of the warriors and found that Diarmuid was missing too. Dimly the king remembered the two young people talking together at the banquet. He had thought nothing of it at the time. But now...

Finn didn't take the news of his **jilting** kindly. "This foolish young warrior has stolen my bride away against her will," roared Finn.

"I doubt that Diarmuid would act with force," replied Cormac. "You yourself know Diarmuid is a man of pure heart and great **integrity.** If he took Grainne away, it would have been at her own request. I'm afraid that my daughter has a strong will of her own."

---

[9] The Wood of the Two Tents is located in western Ireland near Galway.

In a fury, Finn gathered his own warriors, including his son Oisin. Then he led them out of the castle in search of Grainne and Diarmuid. Joined by expert trackers and the best hunting dogs, they followed the couple as far as the wide river. But there they lost the trail.

The warriors could see where the chariot and horse tracks had turned back at the river. In fact the horses—still pulling the chariot—were grazing peacefully in a nearby field.

Finn's son Oisin hoped that the chase would end there. "If these trackers cannot find the trail, it's a useless chase," Oisin told his father. "We may as well return to Tara."

But Finn galloped his horse up and down the river bank and yelled at his trackers in great fury. "You'll find the trail again—and fast!" he roared. "If you don't, I'll hang every one of you right here on the river bank."

At last the trackers hit upon some small footprints beside those of a larger set. Finn and his entire troop of warriors crossed at the ford and took up the chase.

When Finn and the Fionna warriors came to the Wood of the Two Tents, Oisin became worried. "Diarmuid and Grainne must be traveling on foot," he thought. "They can't be far ahead."

Oisin knew the trackers would soon overtake the young couple. How could he warn his friend? Looking around, Oisin saw a hound held on a leash by one of the trackers. It was Finn's own dog.

"Surely Diarmuid has noticed this fine hound during his hunts with the Fionna," Oisin thought. "If he sees it following him through the woods, he will know that Finn is on his trail."

So Oisin took his father's hound and commanded it to follow the fleeing lovers' trail. The great dog dashed off into the woods and disappeared.

At this same time, someone else had become concerned about the fleeing pair. Far away, a powerful magician named Angus stood on his castle wall and stared into the distance. His gray eyes were as mysterious and misty as smoke. His kind, wise brow was creased in a worried frown. Softly, he muttered secret words and spells.

Angus was Diarmuid's foster father.[10] It was he who had brought up Diarmuid to be such a noble and courageous warrior. Angus had raised the boy as his own, and they loved each other dearly.

Now the magician heard a warning in the wind. And he saw a troubling sign in the clouds above the horizon. "Diarmuid is in danger," he thought.

The magician knew he had to act. At his command, the wind lifted him into the air. Angus flew swiftly over the earth toward the Wood of the Two Tents.

Diarmuid had just completed the fence surrounding the hut when he heard something moving in the forest. With one last look at the fence, he quickly shut himself inside.

Diarmuid had built a barrier of sharply pointed saplings. This fence was woven together so tightly that no one could pass through it. In it Diarmuid had built seven narrow doors that could only be opened from the inside.

Looking out through one of his doors, Diarmuid recognized Finn's dog. "Finn is not far away," he said to Grainne, who was hiding in the hut. "His dog has arrived."

Then he spoke gently to the dog, "Here, fellow. I am indeed the one you're after. But I won't hurt you. Come, lie down."

With a wag of his tail, the big dog trotted through the door and lay at Diarmuid's feet.

Diarmuid quickly **donned** his armor and took up his sword. A number of newly made spears lay close at hand.

Diarmuid had no desire to harm Finn or the Fionna warriors. But if any of them tried to climb his fence, he would be ready to kill if he must.

Soon Finn and his men arrived. When they saw the fence, they walked all around it, looking at it carefully.

"Without a doubt, we've found Diarmuid," Finn said to his warriors. "But it would cost us our lives to climb this fence, and I have no desire to lose any of you in a battle such as this. Diarmuid and Grainne will have to come out sooner or

---

[10] It was common in Ireland for men to be raised by a foster father.

later. We'll deal with this young warrior then." So Finn placed his warriors at each of the seven doorways and sat down to wait.

Meanwhile Diarmuid kept watch. As he patrolled the fence, a sudden movement inside the fort startled him. Instantly he leaped to his feet to fight. But then he stopped short as he realized who had so easily entered through his defenses.

"Father!" Diarmuid cried. "You come in time of great need."

The two men greeted each other warmly. Then Diarmuid brought Grainne out of the hut and told his father all that had happened.

Angus looked into Grainne's eyes. "I see you possess some magic yourself," he told her. "And I suspect it was your magic that got my son into this trouble."

Grainne's eyes never **wavered** as she looked at Diarmuid's foster father. "But I like you," he continued. "You're a bold young woman who stands up for herself. I like that. And I think you just might make a fine daughter-in-law."

At these words both Grainne and Diarmuid smiled at each other.

"I love Diarmuid more than life itself," Grainne said to Angus. "I would never wish any harm upon him."

"Come, step under my cloak," Angus said to the lovers. "We can all walk out of here." He lifted his cloak and it swirled upward as though in a breeze.

"Father, I thank you for coming and for your help," said Diarmuid. "But I'm more worried about Grainne's safety than my own. Please, Father, hide her under your cloak and take her out of this place."

"You know I can take you both," Angus said.

"Father, I must stay here. I don't want to spend the rest of my life fleeing Finn."

"Do you want to leave me alone so soon, then?" Grainne demanded.

"No, my love, I don't want that either. I value the life that we can have together. But I will not have Finn blame Angus for my escape. Finn's anger is long-lasting."

Turning to Angus, Diarmuid said, "It will only make trouble for your kingdom, Father, if you take me out of his reach."

"You are right, son," the magician said with a sad smile. "I have no argument with the Fionna. Besides, I wouldn't want to defeat such worthy warriors with my magic. I'll take Grainne to safety and you can escape from Finn on your own."

"If anything should happen to me, you must return Grainne to her own father," Diarmuid said.

The old magician agreed, and they arranged a meeting place. Then Diarmuid looked lovingly at Grainne.

"Please don't worry," he said. "I love you too much to let anything happen to me. I know we'll be together for many years."

"Oh, Diarmuid," Grainne said, embracing him tightly. "Please be careful."

Grainne looked deeply into Diarmuid's eyes. She sensed that some danger followed him. But it wasn't Finn—some other **peril** awaited Diarmuid. Gathering all her courage, she said good-bye.

Then Angus hid Grainne under his cloak, and the two of them safely left the Wood of the Two Tents.

When he was alone, Diarmuid went to one of the doors of his fort. Opening it a small space, he whispered, "Who guards this door?"

"This is Oisin," a familiar voice replied. "You can escape here, Diarmuid. I'll do nothing to stop you."

"No," Diarmuid answered. "I don't want you held responsible for my escape."

Diarmuid went from door to door, asking the same question. At several other doors, friends among the Fionna offered him a chance to slip past them. But each time, Diarmuid refused.

At another door, the trackers stood with their spears. But Diarmuid did not want to escape past the trackers either. Finally, at the seventh door, Diarmuid heard the voice of the

Fionna leader himself.

"Finn guards this door," the warrior declared. "How long will you hide in there like a rabbit, boy?"

Diarmuid kept the door open. "Finn, please let me explain," he began. "I never meant to betray you. But I love Grainne with all my heart. And I truly believe the two of you could never be happy—"

"Enough!" Finn interrupted angrily. "Who are you to decide what makes Grainne happy? I am respected throughout the land. Grainne should have been honored to have a husband like me."

"Can't we talk this over face-to-face?" Diarmuid asked. "Must we fight?"

"You had no right to take her from me!" Finn hissed. "You'll pay for this!"

As Finn moved to open the door wider, Diarmuid shut it in his face. Diarmuid was one of the best warriors in the land, but he wasn't stupid. He knew that Finn would kill him if he ever got inside the fort. Diarmuid would have to escape if he wanted to see his beloved Grainne again.

Taking his longest spear, Diarmuid ran toward the wall where Finn stood guard. Just inside the door, he planted the spear firmly into the ground. With a mighty push, Diarmuid **vaulted** upward. Like a graceful deer, he soared over the wall and over Finn's head.

Finn and his warriors were astonished to see their **quarry** flying over their heads. For a moment, they just stood there in confusion. Diarmuid landed on the ground running and quickly sped out of their reach. He disappeared into the woods so fast that the guards did not even have time to hurl their spears.

Now Finn ordered his men over Diarmuid's fence. Several of the Fionna scaled the fence and opened one of the doors. Finn was confused when he did not find Grainne inside.

"He's tricked me again!" Finn roared in anger. "Doesn't that fool know he won't get away with this? After him! At once!"

But Diarmuid could move very quickly now that he was

traveling alone. Angus had taught his son many secrets of the forest. The young warrior easily lost the trackers and even confused the dogs. By the time Diarmuid joined Angus and Grainne at their meeting place, no one was following him.

Angus and Grainne were overjoyed to see Diarmuid arrive safely. The young princess threw herself into Diarmuid's arms. "I knew you would come," she cried. "I just knew it!"

The three made a campfire and had a small feast to celebrate their escape. They discussed their plans for the future.

"Finn will still follow you," warned Angus. "He will still be angry for some time. But when his hot temper has had a chance to cool off, I'll be able to talk sense into him."

It turned out that the old magician was right. Diarmuid and Grainne found a priest to marry them. Then they spent many months traveling and hiding from the angry Finn. But eventually Angus was able to talk to the leader of the Fionna. Finn agreed to allow Diarmuid and Grainne to go their own way.

After coming to an agreement with Finn, Angus went to talk with Grainne's father. King Cormac was ready to forgive his new son-in-law and his bold daughter. And to make peace, he suggested that Finn marry his other daughter. Everyone readily agreed to that idea. Soon all the wounded feelings seemed to be smoothed over.

Angus did not feel completely secure with the **truce,** however. "Finn's anger has been known to **smolder,**" he warned Diarmuid and Grainne. "It's best if you stay far away from him."

The young lovers agreed. They found some land far away from Finn and Cormac and happily began their life together. They had a stone castle built and ordered crops to be planted in the nearby fields.

As the years went by, Grainne and Diarmuid had four sons. Their lands were rich and the times were peaceful. Everything went well for them, and they were happy.

But eventually Grainne grew lonely. She had lived for many years far away from her childhood home. It had been many years since she had seen her father, and she longed to spend time with him before he died. And, of course, she was aware that Finn was growing older too.

"My love," Grainne said to her husband, "I think that it is time to forget old wounds. My father is an old man, and so is Finn. While they are still here on this earth, we should invite them to our home. Let us all be friends once again."

Diarmuid was not sure he liked the idea. But he finally agreed. So Diarmuid and Grainne planned a great feast. They sent messengers out to invite King Cormac and Finn. Diarmuid and Grainne were joyful when the invitations were accepted.

When Cormac and Finn arrived, many of the Fionna warriors accompanied them.

"Oisin!" Diarmuid said with delight as he spotted his friend. "How good to see you again." He began to think that the feast was a good idea after all.

For her part, Grainne was so happy to see her father that she wept when she embraced him. The old king seemed just as deeply touched to see his daughter again.

Finn, too, behaved in a friendly manner. The old warrior was still strong and active, but his temper had softened somewhat with time. His bitter rage toward the lovers had become mild anger. So the feast proved merry, and there were no arguments among the guests.

The day afterward everything was quiet in the castle of Diarmuid and Grainne. Finn and his Fionna warriors were nowhere to be found. Then Diarmuid heard dogs barking and baying in the woods. He took note of the direction from which the noise came.

"They must have gone to hunt the wild boar that lives on the hill called Ben-Gulben,"[11] Diarmuid said. "That boar is said to be a magnificent beast. I think I'll go and join them."

A feeling of dread suddenly swept over Grainne. "No, my husband, no," Grainne said. "Angus once warned me that you

---

[11] A boar is a fierce wild pig found in Europe. Ben-Gulben is a mountain in Sligo County in western Ireland.

would die from the attack of a wild boar."

"That's foolishness," said Diarmuid. "I've seen many wild boars in the forest. Surely if one of them was going to kill me, it would have done so by now."

"But the boar of Ben-Gulben is larger and more terrible than any other. I suspect that it's a magic creature. I am fearful about this hunt, Diarmuid."

But Diarmuid would not be persuaded to stay at home. He was happy that his problems with Finn seemed to be over. He wanted to be out hunting again with his friends.

So Diarmuid took his weapons and went into the woods. He followed the sound of the baying hounds and was soon climbing Ben-Gulben.

As Diarmuid made his way through the trees, he almost stepped on the dead body of one of the Fionna warriors. It was evident that the man had been slashed by a boar. A little further on, Diarmuid found another warrior who had been killed the same way.

"This boar of Ben-Gulben must be destroyed today," Diarmuid said to himself. "It must never again be allowed to take the life of a brave warrior!"

At the top of the hill, Diarmuid came out of the woods into a clearing. There stood Finn all alone, listening to the sounds of the chase. Somewhere in the woods just beneath him, hounds were baying and men were shouting. Diarmuid could hear the great boar crashing through the underbrush. The sound seemed to come nearer and nearer.

"I have seen the bodies of two Fionna warriors who died under the tusks of the boar of Ben-Gulben," Diarmuid said to Finn. "Let's work together to destroy this beast."

Finn gave Diarmuid a strange look. "Don't you know that you must never hunt a boar?" he asked.

"What do you mean?" asked Diarmuid.

"Your real father once killed an innocent young man. The young man was changed by a druid's spell into a great boar. And that boar was given the task of killing the son of his own murderer. For all you know, my friend Diarmuid, it might be this very boar of Ben-Gulben that seeks to kill you. Go back home and let us kill the deadly beast."

With this warning, Finn walked out of the clearing to continue the hunt. Diarmuid was left alone on the top of the hill. A childhood memory suddenly returned to him.

In his mind Diarmuid could hear the voice of his stepfather. Angus was making him promise never to hunt boar. It had been so long ago that Diarmuid had forgotten it completely. Or was it the magic of the boar that caused him to forget?

Diarmuid didn't have time to give the question much thought. Suddenly, the great boar of Ben-Gulben burst from the trees on the other side of the clearing.

The animal was huge—twice as large as any boar Diarmuid had ever seen. The monstrous beast fixed its small eyes on the warrior. With an angry snort, it dashed at Diarmuid. The beast moved at twice the speed of any other boar.

Diarmuid whipped a spear in front of the charging beast. The point of the spear struck into the animal's shoulder. The boar was slowed, but not for long. It charged again as Diarmuid hurled a second spear. This spear also struck the boar, but with little effect. Though the animal was bleeding from its wounds, it furiously charged on.

Diarmuid drew his sword and held it in front of him. The giant boar dodged the sword and slashed into the warrior's side with his huge tusk. Diarmuid fell back, yelling in pain. With his last ounce of strength, Diarmuid lifted his sword one final time and plunged it into the boar's head. The beast let out a last fearful snort and fell to the ground. In pain and exhaustion, Diarmuid fell beside the beast.

Finn and the Fionna warriors heard the terrible noise of the battle and rushed into the clearing. There they found the Boar of Ben-Gulben dead. And they found the warrior Diarmuid bleeding to death beside him. Finn came and looked down sorrowfully at Diarmuid.

When Diarmuid saw Finn, his face became hopeful. "My friend Finn," Diarmuid said, "you have the power of healing. If you bring me a drink of water in your hands, I will survive this wound."

Finn just stood and gazed at the wounded warrior.

"We've had many good times as warriors and hunters," Diarmuid said, panting for breath. "Remember those times rather than your anger. Give me a drink of water from your own two hands and I will live."

Finn stood motionless, torn by powerful emotions. One expression after another crossed his face, and he seemed unable to move. Then his own son, Oisin, spoke to him.

"My father, it's time to put away your bitterness. Diarmuid is a noble warrior who served you well in days gone by. Give him a drink of water from your own two hands and he will live."

Other Fionna warriors urged their leader to save Diarmuid. Finn looked at the faces of the men he led. Then he silently turned and went to a nearby well. He clasped his hands together and dipped them into the water.

Finn started back toward Diarmuid with the water in his hands. But after taking only a few steps, he let the water spill through his fingers. The old warrior looked up the hill and saw his men waiting there. He saw Diarmuid's pale face **grimace** with pain.

Finn went back to the well and again dipped his hands in the water. He turned to carry the life-saving liquid to Diarmuid.

But then Finn thought of Grainne, and his hands began to shake. Once more, the water spilled to the ground.

The old warrior looked at his men. He saw Diarmuid waiting.

Suddenly Finn knew what he had to do. "I have been a noble and respected warrior all my life," he thought. "But am I really noble? A noble warrior isn't just brave in battle. He is also able to forgive his enemies."

Hurriedly Finn ran back to the well. This time he carried the water all the way back to the fallen hero.

But Finn was too late.

"He's dead," Oisin told Finn.

Finn knelt and looked at the dead warrior's face.

Emotions and memories swirled within him. Finally he rose and looked at Oisin.

"Yes," said Finn simply. Then he turned and walked away.

The Fionna warriors sadly carried the body of Diarmuid back to his wife.

Grainne wept when she saw her lifeless husband. With heavy hearts, Grainne and Angus buried the dead hero. They **mourned** that they hadn't been able to prevent his death.

But Grainne wasn't bitter. She understood that Diarmuid was doomed to die this way. She was happy for the time they had together.

Grainne also bore no hard feelings toward Finn MacCool. Even the most powerful warrior on earth couldn't change the way things were meant to be.

INSIGHTS

Finn MacCool is one of the most popular mythical heroes of Ireland. Although he was human, he did have a bit of the superhuman in him.

For instance, Finn was only eight years old when he took the leadership of the Fionna—the bodyguard of the Irish kings. He obtained it by beheading a fierce monsterlike being whom no one else could conquer.

Legend has it that Finn was superhuman in other ways. He is supposed to have lived to be 230 years old.

Finn also had supernatural wisdom. It is said he received it when he touched the Salmon of Wisdom with his thumb.

This salmon was magical. It was said that the person who touched it first would receive special powers.

As a young man, Finn cooked the fish for his teacher. But since Finn touched it first, it was he who received the gifts of wisdom and foreseeing the future. Afterwards Finn had only to chew on his thumb in order to see into the future.

The Fionna which Finn led was a highly select group. A man who wanted to become a member had to pass some very demanding tests.

For example, one test called for the member-to-be—or "feinnidh"—to stand in a hole in the ground. Nine warriors would encircle him and cast spears at him at the same time. With only a shield and a stick, the feinnidh was supposed to protect himself. If the feinnidh was injured, he was not allowed to join the Fionna.

This wasn't all a feinnidh had to do. In another test, his hair was braided. Then he was ordered to run through the forest with all the Fionna chasing after him.

continued

If the feinnidh was captured during this chase or his weapons shook in his hand, he would be rejected. He was also not accepted if his braided hair had been disturbed by a tree branch or if a dead branch cracked under his foot.

These are just a few of the tough tests a feinnidh had to face. As you might guess, not many who tried out actually became members of the Fionna.

Tara, the castle where Grainne and her father lived, is a well-known place in Ireland. In fact, it was from there that the ancient Irish kings and queens ruled.

Margaret Mitchell, the author of *Gone With the Wind,* may have been inspired by this name. The southern mansion of the central family in her novel is called Tara. And the family who lived there—the O'Haras—are of Irish descent.

The Irish priests were called druids. These druids were powerful members of society. It was their job to smooth things over when the gods became angry. The druids were also respected teachers and magicians.

The word *druid* means "knowledge of the oak." The Irish people held the oak in high esteem. They were even known to worship oak trees in the belief that the trees were gods.

Where did Diarmuid end up after dying? According to the ancient Irish, the dead immediately passed to a land called the Otherworld.

The Otherworld was by no means gloomy. It was a bright, cheerful place where people could do as they pleased and not have to suffer the consequences.

And unlike the society of Fionna warriors, the Otherworld wasn't hard to get into. The Irish believed that all people—both good and evil—would end up in the merry Otherworld.

IZANAMI AND IZANAGI: A CREATION STORY

VOCABULARY PREVIEW

Below is a list of words that appear in the story. Read the list and get to know the words before you read the story.

(set) adrift—let loose without direction
ceremony—service; ritual
collapsed—suddenly fell to the ground
deities—gods
fated—doomed
indecisively—uncertainly; without decision
intruder—invader
maggots—newly hatched insects such as flies
molded—formed
pathetic—poor; worthless
perish—die; pass away
pillar—column, usually used as a support
plead—beg; appeal to
presence—existence; nearness
promised—was likely
revive—bring back to life
scurrying— moving quickly
searing—burning; scorching
surveyed—looked over
tantrums—fits of bad temper

Main Characters

Izanagi—husband of Izanami
Izanami—wife of Izanagi; goddess who helps create islands of Japan and people

IZANAMI AND IZANAGI:
A CREATION STORY

A myth from Japan

The gods Izanami and Izanagi aren't content with their heavenly home. With a fine spirit of adventure, they begin to create many wonderful things on earth. But one day the two gods bring a terrible gift to the world—one that will tear them and every other family apart.

In the beginning heaven and earth were one. As time passed, the lighter, clearer part rose above and became heaven. The heavier, thicker part slowly sank and formed the earth.

Gods and goddesses soon appeared. The two youngest were Izanagi[1]—a god—and Izanami[2]—a goddess. They lived in the heavens like all the other **deities,** but they did not care for it much.

As the young often do, they found home rather dull and wanted to explore other worlds. They were particularly curious about a place far below the heavens known as earth. They stood together on the bridge of heaven—a beautiful rainbow—and looked downward.

"It looks like it's all water," Izanagi said.

Izanami peered into the mists beneath the heavens. "That's all I can see," she answered. "Maybe there's land underneath the water somewhere."

"Let's use a heavenly spear to find out," Izanagi suggested.

The young god and goddess went and fetched a jeweled

[1] (ēz an a´ gē)
[2] (ēz an a´ mē)

spear. They carried it onto the rainbow and poked it deep into the water. When they pulled it out, salty water dripped from the end of the spear.

Then something surprising happened. As the drops fell back into the water, they thickened and formed an island in the ocean.

"There!" said Izanami. "Now we have a place to stand! We can go down and look things over."

Izanagi and Izanami walked all the way down the rainbow and stepped onto the new island. They looked around the land they had just created.

"This is a very fine place," said Izanagi. "Much more interesting than home. I'd rather not go back."

"Then why should we?" said Izanami. "Let's build a home here."

So the god and goddess built a large palace on their new island in the middle of the watery world. They used the lovely jeweled spear as the central **pillar.** When the palace was completed, Izanagi and Izanami stood in the doorway and **surveyed** their new home.

"This will be a lovely place to live," said Izanami

"I've got an idea," said Izanagi. "Let's get married. Let's live here as husband and wife."

"But how do we go about getting married?" asked Izanami.

"I watched two older gods get married once, and I think it's like this," explained Izanagi. "We go in separate directions. Then we meet at the other side of this noble central pillar of our palace. It's simple, isn't it?"

Izanami agreed. "Together, we'll give birth to more islands," she said. "Soon we'll have an entire country to explore."

"You go around from the left," said Izanagi, "and I'll go around from the right."

And so Izanami and Izanagi separated. She went around to the left, and he went around to the right. They met on the far side of the noble pillar that supported their palace.

When they met, Izanami smiled and said, "How

delightful. I've met a lovely young man."

Izanagi smiled and replied, "How delightful. I've met a lovely young woman."

And so Izanagi and Izanami were married. They lived happily together in their palace on the island. After a time, Izanami found herself expecting a child. The young god and goddess were overjoyed. They hoped that Izanami would give birth to an island so that their kingdom would grow.

But the baby that Izanami gave birth to was no island—nor was it a god or goddess. Instead it was a dark and slimy leech child.[3] Izanagi and Izanami were disappointed and couldn't figure out what had gone wrong. How could a god and goddess have given birth to such a **pathetic** baby?

"Perhaps our child will improve with time," said Izanami. But even after three years, the leech child hadn't changed at all. It couldn't even stand up.

To make matters worse, Izanagi and Izanami didn't know how to care for the baby. So Izanami put the leech child into a boat made out of reeds. Then Izanagi took the boat and set it **adrift** on the sea.

"The water is a better place for a such a child," he said.

Izanagi and Izanami wanted to have another child. More than anything else, they wanted to create some beautiful islands so that their kingdom would grow. But they feared that they might give birth to another leech child.

"Why did we produce such an ugly baby instead of a beautiful island?" Izanami asked.

"I think I know why," Izanagi answered. "But I'm not sure you'll like the answer."

"You might as well tell me," said Izanami. "There's no use creating more children until we know what went wrong with the first one."

"The older gods believe it's unlucky for the woman to speak first during the marriage **ceremony,**" said Izanagi. "I believe that's why we produced the leech child."

---

[3] A leech is a soft-bodied worm that sucks another's blood in order to live. A leech child is one who could never survive on his or her own.

"What are you talking about?" asked Izanami.

"It happened when we got married," Izanagi said. "When we met on the other side of the central pillar of our palace, you spoke to me before I spoke to you."

Izanami drew a deep sigh. "So I did," she said. "Well, if you think that's so important, let's just get married all over again."

So Izanagi and Izanami went and stood in the doorway of their palace. They looked at each other and smiled.

"Let us go meet each other at the other side of this noble central pillar of our palace," said Izanagi. "Let us be married and live here as husband and wife."

Izanami just nodded her head in agreement.

"You go around from the left," said Izanagi, "and I'll go around from the right."

And so Izanami and Izanagi separated. She went around to the left, and he went around to the right. They met on the far side of the noble pillar that supported their palace.

When they met, Izanami smiled but said nothing.

This time, Izanagi spoke first. "How delightful," he said, "I've met a lovely young woman."

And only then did Izanami say, "How delightful. I've met a lovely young man."

So the young god and goddess were remarried in the tradition of the older gods. And this time, things went smoothly. As the years went by, Izanami gave birth to eight children—each one healthy and strong. And each of the children turned into a beautiful island. Soon trees and sweet-smelling flowers grew on the new islands. Waterfalls tumbled down the sides of mountains.

Izanagi and Izanami were happy together. They were proud of their new islands. Yet the gods couldn't enjoy the islands because they were covered with a mist that rose from the sea.

"Our children are lovely, but we can barely see them," said Izanami. "This mist is annoying."

"I agree," said Izanagi. "We need a helper to take care of this problem."

So Izanagi took a puff of his own breath and shaped it into a little god—the god of the wind. The wind blew away the mist until all the islands sparkled like jewels in the ocean.

Then Izanagi and Izanami watched and laughed while the wind blew the young islands around. He shaped and arranged them perfectly on the surface of the water.

"Our little god of the wind is not as powerful as we are, but he does his job very well," said Izanami.

"Yes, he does," said Izanagi. "And we have lots of tasks for other such helpers to do."

So Izanagi and Izanami created gods and goddesses to watch over the mountains, streams, trees, fruits, and flowers. They created gods and goddesses for the seas, waterfalls, rocks, and everything else that appeared on the earth. None of these deities had the power of Izanami and Izanagi. But they made earthly things even better than before.

Then the couple **molded** the first people. When they were finished, the god and goddess admired the new human beings.

"They can enjoy the islands just as much as we do," Izanami said.

"Yes," replied Izanagi. "These people will see the wonders we have created and worship us forever."

Izanami and Izanagi meant for humans to live forever. For this reason, birth and death were unknown. There wasn't even a word for death.

Then Izanami gave birth to another child—the most beautiful child of all. The baby girl gave off a warm bright light. The proud parents named her Amaterasu.[4] Izanami and Izanagi quickly realized that Amaterasu would grow into an extraordinary goddess.

"Amaterasu must live in a special place," said Izanami. "She's too important to keep here on a little island."

"You're right," said Izanagi. "Amaterasu deserves to live in the heavens. From there, she can look down upon our beautiful islands."

So Izanagi and Izanami took Amaterasu to the foot of the

---

[4] (am at er a´ soo)

rainbow. Then they showed her how to walk up the rainbow to the heavens.

Amaterasu waved a cheerful good-bye to her parents and took her place in the heavens. She became the sun, which sends out warmth and light to the entire world.

Izanagi and Izanami stood on their island, looking up at their youngest child with great pride.

"Amaterasu will be the most powerful of our gods and goddesses," said Izanagi.

"Yes, and she'll give birth to a race of emperors to rule the islands,"[5] said Izanami.

So the couple continued to live happily in their island palace. After a time, Izanami gave birth to a god who was almost as beautiful as Amaterasu. He shone with a soft light. And like Amaterasu, he too **promised** to be very special.

"This child would make a fine companion for Amaterasu," said Izanami.

Izanagi agreed. So Izanagi and Izanami took their new child to the foot of the rainbow and sent him up to the heavens. Soon the moon—for that was the young god's name—was shining down from his place in the heavens. After a time, the moon god and the sun goddess became husband and wife.

Izanami gave birth to many other gods, some more troublesome than others. The storm god, for example, sometimes had temper **tantrums.**

But it was Izanami's last child—the god of fire—who caused the greatest grief. This god came into the world already **searing** hot. As a result, Izanami was badly burned while giving birth to him. Indeed, Izanami became so ill with fever that she couldn't move.

Izanagi tended Izanami as best he could. He brought her water and helped her drink. But his wife became weaker and weaker.

Finally Izanami closed her eyes and stopped breathing.

---

[5] The islands in this story are modern-day Japan. The emperors are believed to be direct descendants of Amaterasu.

She had died. Izanagi didn't understand what had happened. His wife's death was the first in the world.

After several unsuccessful attempts to **revive** his wife, Izanagi grew furious. He drew his sword and attacked the baby god of fire, striking him two times. But the fire god wasn't harmed. In fact, the young god just divided into three tiny deities.

"Why should Izanami die when I can't even harm the fire god?" cried Izanagi with despair. "It isn't fair!"

But fair or not, Izanagi realized it was no use striking out against his children. He let the three fire gods go their own way into the world.

Izanami herself was drawn down into the land of darkness—a place called Yomi.[6] This land was dark and eerie—far different from the brightly lit islands on earth. Izanami didn't like it at all.

"I hope that Izanagi comes for me soon," said Izanami after she crossed Yomi Pass—the gate to the underworld. "It's dark and lonely down here."

Izanami knew she didn't necessarily have to stay in Yomi. Her husband could come down to rescue her and return her to the land of the living.

But there was a catch—Izanami knew she must not taste any of the food of Yomi. If she took just one bite, she would be **fated** to spend the rest of eternity in darkness.

At first Izanami was not interested in food or drink. She missed Izanagi too much. Soon, though, she began to feel hungry.

"Izanagi, where are you?" Izanami wondered. "Surely you haven't forgotten me?" The goddess wandered through the darkness, feeling more and more hungry. How long could she wait before breaking down and eating?

Izanami spied some Yomi food nearby. It certainly didn't look very appetizing. But the hungry goddess was growing desperate.

"I've been down here for a long time," she thought. "I

[6] (yō´ mē)

might as well accept the fact that Izanagi will never come to rescue me." Slowly she walked toward the food.

Meanwhile, back on earth, Izanami's husband remained miserably unhappy. All alone, he paced through the beautiful palace and about the island where he and Izanami had once lived in such happiness. The waterfalls, streams, and trees all sang to him. The gods and goddesses of nature tried to cheer their father up. But Izanagi only became lonelier and sadder.

No one knows why Izanagi waited so long to go after his wife. But finally he could no longer live without her. He decided to follow her into the land of darkness and bring her back to the land of the living. So he set out on the road to Yomi.

The path was long and difficult. Izanagi didn't know how many days he walked. Each day, there was less light to see by. It got so dark that he had to feel his way carefully with each foot to be sure he was still on the path. Finally he sensed Izanami's **presence** in the surrounding darkness.

"Where are you, Izanami?" he called. "I know you're here somewhere!"

But he received no answer. Even so, he knew that she could not be far in front of him.

Izanagi walked deeper and deeper into the land of Yomi, calling Izanami's name again and again. He grew desperate and began to **plead** with the darkness.

"Izanami, I know you're nearby," he said softly. "I love you. I've come a long and difficult way to find you. Why won't you answer me?"

"Izanagi," a voice whispered. Izanagi knew it was his wife's voice. But she didn't sound happy. The whisper shaped itself into a long, sad sigh.

Despite Izanami's sad tone, Izanagi was greatly cheered to hear her voice.

"Izanami, my beloved wife," he said, "I have come to take you back with me. I cannot be happy without you."

"Izanagi!" the voice replied sharply. "Why did you wait so long?"

Izanagi was shocked at the anger in Izanami's voice. He'd

thought that she would be happy that he had sought her out.

"What's wrong, Izanami?" he said. "Why don't you come to me? Surely you don't want to remain here in the dark."

"I waited for you. I even refused to eat anything here in Yomi," said Izanami. "I hoped to return to the land of the living."

"And now?" Izanagi asked, his heart sinking.

"Now I have no choice," Izanami said bitterly. "I have eaten the food of Yomi, so I can never return to the light. I must stay here forever."

"Don't be foolish. You can still return with me."

"You must neither touch me nor set eyes on me. You must return immediately to the land of the living. Please, Izanagi, listen to me. Go back to your own world at once."

But Izanagi was not satisfied. He could not bear to be so close to Izanami, to hear her voice, and yet to leave without her. He reached into his hair and withdrew a many-toothed comb.[7] He broke off a tooth, then put the comb back into his hair. Holding the tooth of the comb in his hand, he lit it and held it up like a torch.

Izanagi was so shocked at what he saw that he almost dropped his torch. In the sudden glare he saw how Izanami's body had already started to decay. Her rotting flesh was falling away from her bones. **Maggots** were crawling all over her, feeding on what was left of her body. Izanagi cried out and turned his eyes away.

Izanami was furious. "You have shamed me!" she shrieked. "This is no act of love. Why didn't you do as I asked? Why did you have to look at me, foolish man?"

Izanagi tried to stammer out an apology, but he was too horrified to speak. Instead he turned to leave.

"You shall be punished for your thoughtlessness!" Izanami screamed. And she called for help from the land of the dead.

In response to Izanami's screams, many terrible shapes

---

[7] In Japanese society, it was customary for both men and women to wear fancy combs in their hair.

appeared out of the darkness. These were the terrible women of Yomi, horrible monsters of death. When they saw Izanagi, they crept toward him.

"Destroy the **intruder!**" hissed one of the terrible women.

"Catch him before he escapes!" cried another.

Izanagi backed away from the monsters. He turned to run, but now his torch had burned out. As he staggered along the darkened path, Izanagi heard the horrible creatures hissing and **scurrying** behind him. They knew their way better than he did and were sure to catch him.

Izanagi pulled the comb from his hair again. He thought, "If I use a piece of this as a torch again, I will be able to find my way more easily. But the monsters will also find *me* more easily."

Izanagi stood on the path for a moment, clutching the comb **indecisively.** At a loss as to what to do, he threw his comb to the ground in front of the monsters who followed him. Surprisingly, the comb turned into a garden of green, juicy bamboo shoots.

The horrible women had never seen such plants in the land of Yomi. Curious, they stopped to taste the bamboo shoots. Before long, they were arguing and fighting over every bite.

While the monsters were busy with the bamboo, Izanagi carefully felt his way along the dark path. At last, it seemed as though he was leaving the darkness behind.

Izanagi stopped and rubbed his eyes. Yes, he was now able to see the faintest shades of gray. But soon he heard the monsters of Yomi close behind him again. Surely they would catch him before he could escape this terrible world!

"The bamboo shoots delayed them for a short time," Izanagi thought. "What can I offer that will stop them again?"

Izanagi pulled off his black headdress and threw it to the ground. The headdress changed to a bunch of fresh grapes. As they had with the bamboo shoots, the horrible women stopped to eat and fight over each and every grape.

By the time the monsters caught up with Izanagi again, he had reached the land of the living. Izanagi rolled a huge rock across Yomi Pass, blocking the monsters' way.

Izanagi **collapsed** on his side of the boulder. As exhausted as he was, he was relieved to have escaped the horrible land of Yomi. But he was sad that he had hurt Izanami's feelings and had lost her forever.

Then he heard a familiar voice speaking from the other side of the boulder. It was Izanami—and she still sounded furious.

"Izanagi, you have shamed me!" she shouted. "I will revenge myself by killing every one of your people. I have already ordered that they be destroyed. I can strangle a thousand every day, and soon they will all be gone."

"Izanami, have you forgotten that they are your people, too?" Izanagi asked tiredly and sadly. "For your sake as well as mine, I will not let you take this revenge. I will more than replace any people you destroy. I now order a thousand a day to be born—plus half a thousand more. I will not let the people of our islands **perish."**

Then came a long silence as Izanagi and Izanami both realized that they had created something new. They had brought death and birth to their beloved island people. This was their final and most wonderful creation.

Finally Izanami spoke again. This time her voice was quiet and warm—more like it was in happier days.

"My husband, my love, my lord Izanagi," she said, "you must accept my death. Please don't try to bring me back from Yomi. We must never meet again."

"I will honor your wishes," said Izanagi. "Our marriage is ended."

And so Izanami went back down into the land of Yomi. And Izanagi went and washed in the sea to rid himself of the stains of the land of death. Then he returned to the palace.

Ever after that, Izanagi often thought of Izanami when he looked at the islands, trees, waterfalls, rocks, flowers, people—all the countless things they had created together.

Often he pictured Izanami when he remembered the special gifts they had given humankind—marriage and separation, birth and death. Theirs was a splendid creation.

And in a mysterious way, their separation was the most important part of it all.

INSIGHTS

Like the gods of many other cultures, Izanagi and Izanami were human in appearance. But unlike other gods, Japanese gods were not all-knowing. When they were in heaven, they had no idea what was happening down on earth. They had to rely on messengers to bring them information.

The Japanese gods possessed two souls—one gentle and one violent. The actions of a god depended on which soul was in control at the time. This may explain Izanami's violent attack on her husband. It may also account for the argument that developed between the sun and moon.

As mentioned in the myth of Izanagi and Izanami, the moon god and the sun goddess married. However, one day the moon grew upset with the goddess of food and killed her.

The sun was so enraged by this that she insisted on separating from the moon. In fact, she refused to ever look at her husband again. This story explains why the sun rules the day while the moon guards the night.

Izanami and Izanagi used a jeweled spear as the main support of their palace. Even today the central pillar of a house is often an object of honor—not only in Japan, but in many other countries as well.

The marriage rite of Izanami and Izanagi also reflects a tradition that is found around the world. In many cultures the bride and groom walk around a fire, tree, or other object as part of the wedding ceremony.

Izanami is unable to leave Yomi once she eats food in the underworld.

continued

The idea of food that entraps the dead isn't unique to the Japanese. In one Greek myth, a goddess named Persephone is unable to return to earth because she tasted a fruit in the underworld.

Like Izanami, Izanagi also eventually died. However, he didn't go to Yomi. In fact, there is disagreement on just where he went. Some myths hold that after dying, Izanagi hid himself on a desert island, never to be seen again. Still other stories say that Izanagi returned to his original home in heaven with the other gods.

Japanese mythology tells us little about Yomi, the land of the dead. We do know that wicked beings lived there. And the demons that inhabited Yomi were not nearly as powerful as the gods in heaven.

And what was the land of the gods like? It's said that it was a beautiful place—very much like Japan itself. One got there by crossing a heavenly river called Ama no Gawa.

One myth tells how earth used to be linked to heaven by a bridge. But one day all the gods happened to be sleeping on it at the same time. Their combined weight caused the bridge to collapse. Thus the path to heaven is not as easy as it once was.

This myth reflects the Shinto belief system. Shinto is the original religion of Japan.

Izanagi and Izanami's many children became the gods and goddesses in the Shinto pantheon. (A *pantheon* is all the gods and goddesses worshipped by a people.) There are as many as eight million gods and goddesses in that pantheon. The number isn't so surprising if you keep in mind that many lakes, mountains, and trees in Japan have their own spirit—or kami.

Izanagi demonstrates another Shinto belief in this myth when he cleanses himself after returning from Yomi. His action reflects a typical Shinto concern for purity. Death and anything to do with it were believed to be unclean. So naturally after a funeral, the family of the dead person wash themselves with water.

RAMA AND SITA

VOCABULARY PREVIEW

Below is a list of words that appear in the story. Read the list and get to know the words before you start the story.

apprehensive—nervous; troubled
banish—cast out
boundless—without limit
canopy—covering
conduct—manage; direct
crafty—clever; sly
cringing—fearful; weak-hearted
distressed—worried; upset
elated—delighted; overjoyed
engaging—clashing; battling
exile—separation or removal from one's home or country
fidelity—loyalty; faithfulness
forlorn—very unhappy; miserable
hermit—one who lives alone, often in the wilderness and usually for religious reasons
humiliation—shame; dishonor
oath—pledge; promise
obligingly—agreeably; willingly
regal—kingly; royal
unwittingly—unknowingly; without meaning to
wielded—used; handled

Main Characters

Bharata—son of Dasa-ratha and Kaikeyi

Dasa-ratha—king of Ayodhya; father of Rama and Rama's brothers

Hanuman—Sugriva's advisor

Kaikeyi—one of Dasa-ratha's three wives; mother of Bharata

Kumbha-karna—brother of Ravana

Lakshmana—Rama's faithful brother

Rakshas—wild demons; warriors of the jungle

Rama—exiled king of Ayodhya

Ravana—king of the Rakshas

Sita—Rama's wife

Sugriva—king of the monkeys

Surpa-Nakha—Raksha princess

Vibhishana—brother of Ravana

Rama and Sita

A Hindu myth from India

Rama is a king without a throne and a warrior general without an army. The only things left to him are his lovely wife, faithful brother, and humble jungle home. But even those things are threatened when Rama accidentally offends a savage king.

*R*ama! Rama, wait!"

At the sound of the distant voice, three people turned and peered through the dense jungle growth. One of them was Rama,[1] the prince of Ayodhya.[2] With him were his wife Sita and his brother Lakshmana.[3]

"Who can be calling me?" Rama wondered. He looked at his two companions, who shook their heads. They were as confused as he was.

"Rama!" they heard again. As the three looked in the direction of the voice, they at last spotted a man running toward them.

"Bharata!"[4] said Rama in surprise. "Why are you here,

[1] (rahm *or* ra´ ma)
[2] (a yō´ dē a)
[3] (sē´ ta) (lock shman´ *or* lock shma´ na)
[4] (bar´ at *or* ba ra´ ta)

brother? Why aren't you at home preparing to rule our father's kingdom?"

"Rama," said Bharata, panting. "I come with important news. Your **exile** is over! You can return to Ayodhya immediately and take the throne."

Before Rama could answer, his brother Lakshmana broke in. "How so, Bharata? What about the promises our father made to your mother, Kaikeyi?[5] Didn't he promise to make you king? And didn't Kaikeyi make him **banish** his favorite son to the jungle?"

Bharata lowered his dark eyes. "I'm sorry to report that our father is dead. He died of grief. He wished he'd never made those promises to my mother."

Then Bharata looked at Rama. "Rama, my mother has changed. She now sees that the promise she forced from our father was wrong. She agrees that, as the eldest son, you have the right to the throne, not I."

As Rama listened to his brother, his thoughts turned toward home. It was hard to imagine that his father was dead. King Dasa-ratha[6] had been a wise and fair ruler, and the people loved him. He had also tried to be fair to his three wives. But it was his favorite wife, Kaikeyi, who had caused all this trouble.

When the king decided to retire, Kaikeyi was happy. After all, her husband was growing old, and he deserved to rest.

But then Kaikeyi heard that her husband was about to appoint his eldest son, Rama, as the new king. She became fiercely jealous.

Kaikeyi wanted her own son Bharata to be the new ruler. So she took advantage of the fact that Dasa-ratha had promised her two favors.

"First, I want my son Bharata appointed king," she declared to her husband. "And not only that. I want you to banish Rama to the jungle for fourteen years!"

Poor Dasa-ratha. He had given his word. And if he went

[5] (keh kā ē *or* ka ēk´ u yē)
[6] (dash rat´ *or* dash´ a rath´ a)

back on his promise, he would lose the respect of his people. The **distressed** king was forced to give in.

Rama, being a model son, took the news well. Obeying his father was more important to him than becoming king. So he immediately packed his things and set off into the jungle. Rama's wife Sita and brother Lakshmana—ever loyal to the prince—insisted on accompanying him during his exile.

Rama brought his attention back to the present. "Bharata, you know I can't go back. My father's **oath** holds true—even in death. So here in the jungle I must stay."

Rama looked at Sita and Lakshmana. "I know that you two are determined to stay with me during my exile," he said. "But you still have a chance to turn back. You can both return to Ayodhya."

Sita, a beautiful woman with long black hair, shook her head. "Rama, as your wife, it's my duty to stay by your side— no matter what. My feelings haven't changed. I'm staying with you."

Lakshmana, a strong young warrior, felt the same. "Brother, there are many dangers here in the jungle. You need someone to back you up. I'm staying with you as well."

Rama turned back to Bharata. "Well, there you are. I'm sorry you've journeyed through the jungle for nothing. But I cannot return to Ayodhya."

"But your exile has barely begun! And our people need your wisdom and your strong hand now!" cried Bharata.

Rama was firm. "Go and rule in my place," he told Bharata. "No matter what you say, I will not dishonor my father's memory by ignoring his promise."

Stubbornly, Bharata said, "I will go back to Ayodhya, but I will not rule. Before I leave, let me have your sandals."

"Why?" asked Rama with surprise.

"Just give them to me, and I'll explain."

Rama **obligingly** took off his sandals and handed them to his brother.

"Meet Ayodhya's new king!" exclaimed Bharata, holding up the sandals. "I will put these on the throne in your place, Rama. Whenever you think of your kingdom, remember that it will be ruled by a pair of shoes until you return!" Bharata then said his farewells and returned to Ayodhya.

For days, the three exiles roamed the wilderness. Deeper and deeper into the jungle they went. But search as they might, they couldn't find a good place to settle.

Along the way, a wise old **hermit** crossed their path. The hermit greeted Rama. "I can tell by your face that you're a true hero!" he exclaimed. "I have a gift for you!"

As the exiles watched, the hermit gave Rama a magic weapon. "I give you the bow of Vishnu,"[7] he declared. "Here also is a quiver[8] of arrows made by the gods themselves. Take care of these. You will need them one day."

"Thank you for the fine weapon," Rama replied. "It's comforting to know the gods are with us."

The exiles bid farewell to the hermit and continued looking for a place to live. One day, the exiles found themselves in a beautiful clearing. It seemed the perfect spot to settle. So there Lakshmana and Rama built a bamboo house. Finally these three noble people had a jungle home.

Wise old hermits visited from time to time and taught Rama good and useful things. Rama and his companions also learned the ways and speech of animals.

Still, the three of them were a little bored. They missed being part of the busy palace life.

"Here we are in the deepest jungle, and there's nothing exciting to do," complained Lakshmana. He looked up at the sky as if in appeal to the gods. "Please, send us a little adventure!"

Little did Lakshmana know his prayers were soon to be answered.

It all began when the hermits complained of being attacked and robbed by strange-looking beings called Rakshas. Rama and Lakshmana were curious about these Rakshas.

"Rakshas," one hermit explained, "are fierce warrior

[7] Vishnu is a major Hindu god. He is the preserver of earthly life.
[8] A quiver is a case for holding arrows.

creatures. One can barely see them as they flit from tree to tree. They can change their shapes at will and they use evil magic."

"Where do they live?" Rama asked.

The hermit shrugged and said, "The trees, the ground, the bushes—anywhere at all."

"How many of them are there?" asked Lakshmana.

"Who can tell?" the hermit said. "They are part of the wilderness itself. No one can count them."

Rama and Lakshmana decided to watch over the hermits. They often stepped in to defend the hermits from the attacking Rakshas. The brothers found it easy to drive away the strange creatures.

"Some warriors these are!" chuckled Rama.

"Such evil power too!" replied Lakshmana.

They laughed at the very idea that the Rakshas might be the least bit magical. But they would soon regret not taking them more seriously.

One day, a Raksha princess named Surpa-Nakha[9] was wandering through the jungle with her brothers. At the sight of the bamboo home in the clearing she stopped and stared in fascination.

"Go ahead without me," Surpa-Nakha said to her brothers. "I want to find out more about these odd people who dare to live in my wilderness."

But once Surpa-Nakha saw Rama, she became enchanted by his beauty. She had never seen anyone so tall, pale, and **regal.** The Raksha princess left her hiding place and approached the exiled prince.

"Who are you, warrior?" she asked. "Why are you here in my jungle? Why do you live in this strange house? And where did you get your mighty bow, your quiver and arrows?"

Rama found the strange, wild woman entertaining. In fact, he could barely keep from laughing at her comical looks and odd ways. But he politely related the entire story of why he and his wife and brother were living in the jungle. Then he

---

[9] (soorp na ka´ *or* soor´ pa na ka´)

asked the jungle woman who she was.

"I am Surpa-Nakha," she answered boldly. "I roam this jungle as freely as I wish."

The Raksha woman then walked into the bamboo house and began to look around. Though Sita was sitting in plain view, Surpa-Nakha paid no attention to her. The brothers watched Surpa-Nakha in amusement. She reminded them of a small monkey whose curiosity had brought it into their home.

But then Surpa-Nakha did something which really surprised the brothers. She stopped her curious poking around and stood before Rama. She spoke daringly—and very seriously.

"I am a powerful princess," Surpa-Nakha told Rama. "I have great magic. My kingdom is **boundless.** You are not nearly as powerful as I am. Even so, I think I'll take you for my husband."

Rama stared at the jungle princess, not quite sure how to react. "As you can see, I already have one wife," he said, trying not to laugh.

"Your human wife is no match for me," Surpa-Nakha said sternly. "Put her aside at once. You should be honored that I have taken an interest in you."

Now Rama couldn't help but show his amusement. "No, Surpa-Nakha," he said with a grin. "I'm forever bound to Sita. And you would not be happy as my second wife. Why don't you ask my brother instead? Lakshmana is all alone in this jungle home."

The Raksha princess looked at Rama in confusion. Was he really daring to reject her?

Lakshmana quickly picked up Rama's playful spirit. "Oh no, Surpa-Nakha," he said teasingly. "You would not want me for a husband. I'm no more than a slave to these other two. You're a fine princess and could never marry a slave."

Then Surpa-Nakha realized that the two men were mocking her. Never in her life had she been treated with disrespect. Never before had her pride been wounded.

"How dare you insult me!" she shrieked. "Who do you think I am? Do you think me weak and powerless?"

With those words, the little jungle princess darted wildly across the room toward Sita. Surpa-Nakha seemed to grow taller, and magic crackled in the air around her. The gentle Sita grew pale and trembled before the wild woman's magic.

Surpa-Nakha laughed at Sita's fear. She turned again to Rama and shouted, "Do you prefer this **cringing** human woman to me? Very well, then. You shall have her dead body as your companion!"

Rama now saw the danger he had **unwittingly** caused. He swiftly leapt between the two women. Standing protectively in front of Sita, he cried, "Help me, Lakshmana!"

Lakshmana charged across the room and grabbed Surpa-Nakha's hair. He snatched her away. Quickly he whipped out his sharp knife and yanked the wild woman's head back. Before Surpa-Nakha could react, Lakshmana had sliced off the tip of her nose. Then, with two quick flicks of his knife, he slit both her ears.

The Raksha woman ran bleeding and screaming from the house and vanished into the jungle. Rama could still hear her cries of pain and fury as he bent to take care of his wife.

Sita was shaken by Surpa-Nakha's magic. But she soon began to regain her strength.

"My sense of humor has gotten us into trouble," Rama said to his wife and brother. "I'm sorry for that. What will happen next?"

The Raksha woman's cries had scarcely died away when Rama and Lakshmana became aware of strange sounds of movement in the jungle. Shadows slid from tree to tree, and the vines shivered as though in an icy breeze. The **canopy** of trees seemed to close overhead, making the jungle even darker than usual.

"What's going on?" wondered Rama.

He didn't have to wait long to find out. Raksha warriors had heard of their princess' pain and **humiliation.** They were now gathering to engage in war against Rama and Lakshmana.

As well-trained warriors, the two brothers could scent a coming battle. Rama took up the powerful bow of Vishnu with its quiver and arrows. Lakshmana grabbed two mighty swords. Then the brothers stood side by side, waiting for the attack to begin.

Shadowy forms poured out of the jungle and started the attack. Soon the Rakshas and exiles were **engaging** sword with sword and returning arrow for arrow.

It was a fierce battle. The air snapped with sparks, as though lightning were dancing under the dark trees. All the jungle animals and birds fled from the battle. The entire jungle shook and groaned from the destruction.

The brothers never really saw their attackers. Nor did they know how many Raksha warriors they fought. At times they believed thousands of Rakshas thundered through the jungle toward the bamboo house.

"Where are they all coming from?" Rama shouted to Lakshmana.

Rama's brother shook his head. "They seem to appear out of thin air!" he replied.

Time also flowed strangely. Did days or weeks of fighting pass? The brothers couldn't tell.

Rama and Lakshmana fought on against the mysteriously shifting shapes of the enemy. The brothers **wielded** their weapons with skill and strength. They held firm even in the face of the demons' most terrible spells. Vishnu's bow could not miss while Rama handled it. And Lakshmana's swords cut through flesh and magic alike.

Throughout the battle, Sita hid in the bamboo house. Though she trembled with fear, she had faith in Rama and Lakshmana. She was certain they would defeat the Rakshas.

At long last the wilderness became quiet again. Rama and Lakshmana stood exhausted but unharmed in the jungle clearing.

"Listen," said Rama softly.

"What? I don't hear anything," replied Lakshmana.

"That's what I mean," said Rama. "Surely we didn't kill *all* the Rakshas. Where did they go? They must live somewhere."

"Surpa-Nakha said that she was a princess," Lakshmana

said. "Where there's a princess, there must be a king."

"And where there's a king, there's a kingdom," replied his brother. "The only question is where?"

The brothers were right—the Rakshas did indeed have a king. His name was Ravana[10] and he was Surpa-Nakha's brother. He ruled the Rakshas from his palace in the kingdom of Lanka.[11]

Ravana was furious when he saw what had happened to his sister's nose and ears. After listening to her story, Ravana thought long and hard. He had to come up with a way to destroy Rama.

It was not only his sister he wanted to avenge. Rama and Lakshmana had also killed Ravana's brother and countless other warriors during the battle.

"Rama will pay for this," Ravana murmured angrily. He closed his eyes and thought some more.

"I have it," Ravana decided at last. "I will seize his most prized possession. Yes, I will capture his wife Sita and bring her to my palace!"

❖   ❖   ❖

Not long after the battle, Lakshmana and Sita were out walking near their jungle home. Suddenly Sita spotted a deer drinking from a stream nearby.

As the deer raised its head, Sita gasped at the sapphires set in its antlers. The jewels glowed brightly in the sunlight. As the deer turned and faced Sita, she glimpsed the shine of its silky coat. Sita took a step closer, and the deer looked directly into her eyes.

"What a beautiful deer!" Sita said in wonder. "I just have to have it for my own."

But when she moved closer, the deer gracefully leapt the stream and disappeared into the trees. Sita drew a deep, sad sigh. She had been fascinated by the beautiful animal.

Lakshmana ran up beside Sita. He had seen the deer too.

[10] (ra van´ *or* ra va´ na)

[11] Lanka is now known as Sri Lanka. (Until 1972 it was called Ceylon.) It is an island nation off the southeast coast of India.

But worry rather than wonder showed on his face.

"Oh, Lakshmana, won't you catch it for me?" Sita begged. "What a marvelous pet it would make!"

Lakshmana knew something was wrong. "Forget about the deer, Sita," he said. "It's long gone by now."

But Sita could not get the magic deer out of her mind. That night, she described it to Rama and begged him to capture it for her.

"Please, Rama," she said. "It's not very often I ask for anything, but I really must have this deer! It seems just a little thing to do after all your mighty deeds."

Before Rama could answer, Lakshmana spoke up. "This cannot be an ordinary deer. Its coat is like fine silk, and it has sapphires in its antlers. Why would a deer like that be freely roaming the jungle? No, that animal is magic—and its magic is probably evil."

"Something so beautiful can't be evil," Sita insisted. "You can tell that it's a royal creature. And such a fine animal doesn't belong in this wilderness. Its true home is in a palace garden."

"Don't forget that the Rakshas can change their shapes," said Lakshmana. "As lovely as it seems, this deer could be a magic warrior. It wouldn't be wise to bring a thing like that into our home."

But Sita was still enchanted by the jeweled deer. "If you cannot capture it," she pleaded, "then kill it and bring me its skin and antlers. It would make a rug finer than any in the kingdom. Rama, I must have this deer, one way or the other."

Rama had said nothing during this argument. By his wife's description of the deer, he knew it was no ordinary creature.

"Is Sita right?" Rama wondered. "Does this creature deserve a life in a palace garden? Or is Lakshmana correct in saying it's a Raksha magician in disguise?"

Rama didn't know. But whichever was the case, he decided to track the animal down.

The next morning Rama took up his bow and quiver of arrows. "Stay close to Sita and watch over her," he told

Lakshmana. "There's something about Sita's attachment to this magic deer that worries me."

"I'm glad you feel that way too," Lakshmana replied. "I promise to keep Sita safe. In return, you must promise to be very careful."

Rama easily found the tracks of the beautiful deer and followed them deep into the jungle. From time to time he caught a glimpse of the animal. He could see it was as beautiful as Sita had claimed. But try as he might, he could not get close to it.

The deer led Rama farther and farther away from his wife and brother and their jungle home. But just when Rama thought he had lost it completely, the deer would appear again. The creature seemed to be playing a game with him.

Finally Rama felt **apprehensive** about being away from his companions so long. He did not believe he could capture the deer alive. So he placed an arrow in the bow of Vishnu. The next time he glimpsed the deer, Rama shot at it. The arrow struck its target, and the deer fell to the ground.

Rama approached the deer and found it dying. The strange creature seemed to flicker like a flame. It looked like a Raksha one second and a deer the next. Rama stood and watched in silence, wondering what to do.

"Sita will be upset if I don't bring the deer back," he said to himself. "But what if the animal was sent to bring us harm?"

Rama's thoughts were interrupted by a strange sound coming from the deer. The dying creature suddenly raised its head and called out in a piercing human voice. The sound of its outcry made Rama's skin crawl.

"Lakshmana, help me!" the deer cried. "I'm wounded! I'm dying here in the jungle! Help me!"

With those words, the deer lowered its head and died.

"Why did the deer's words frighten me so?" Rama wondered aloud. Then he realized the truth. "Its voice!" whispered Rama in horror. "Its voice was exactly like mine! I've been tricked by the Rakshas!"

The deer's piercing voice echoed throughout the jungle.

At last it reached the clearing, where Lakshmana and Sita awaited Rama's return. But it didn't seem far away. It sounded very near.

At the sound of the magic deer's cry, Sita gasped and clutched Lakshmana's arm.

"Go quickly!" she said.

But Lakshmana did not move. "I don't believe it," he replied. "It must be another Raksha trick. I promised Rama that I would stay and guard you."

"You claim to love your brother," Sita cried furiously. "Didn't you hear him call? Go to his aid at once!"

"Rama has never been defeated," insisted Lakshmana. "Surely you don't think that deer got the best of him?"

"Betrayer!" screamed Sita, her eyes blazing. "My husband is wounded and bleeding. And didn't you hear how close he sounded? He must be just beyond those trees! Will you let him die right within your reach?"

Lakshmana was deeply hurt by Sita's words, but he didn't know what to do. He felt sure the cry had been some kind of trick. Even so, it had certainly sounded like Rama's voice. How could he be certain his brother was not in desperate danger? Lakshmana took up his sword and rushed into the jungle.

But when Lakshmana reached the nearest trees, he saw no sign of Rama.

"Strange," he murmured aloud. "The voice sounded so near! Maybe just a little farther…"

So Lakshmana continued deeper and deeper into the wilderness in search of Rama.

In the meantime, Sita paced back and forth in front of the bamboo house. When she grew tired, she sat and listened carefully for the slightest sound. But for quite some time, there was nothing to be heard but the jungle breeze and the cries of the animals.

Sita closed her eyes and lowered her head—not in weariness but despair. "I was wrong!" she said, beginning to cry. "Oh, how I wish I had not asked either of them to leave! It was my selfishness that caused this."

A sound reached Sita's ears. She raised her head and leapt to her feet with joy.

But it was not Lakshmana and Rama standing before her. It was only an old hermit.

Disappointed as she was, Sita was glad to see a friendly face—and she was sure she could trust the jungle hermits. She politely offered him water and bread.

Sita was unaware that the jungle had suddenly grown silent. And she didn't notice that the birds and beasts seemed to be waiting breathlessly and fearfully. Even the trees and vines didn't move in the breeze.

The hermit looked all around. He studied the thatched roof[12] of the bamboo house.

"Why do you live here?" he asked Sita. "You are obviously of noble blood. Why don't you have a husband who can provide you with a palace?"

"I am proud to be the wife of Rama," Sita answered, holding her head high. "He's a hero and a godlike man. What more should a woman desire?"

"A true king," cried the hermit, leaping to his feet. "A true king such as me!"

The hermit's shape flickered wildly for a moment. In a flash, he took the form of a Raksha—a Raksha king, that is. For King Ravana had come to complete the next step of his plan.

Sita tried to run, but Ravana laughed and caught her by her long dark hair. Sita winced in pain. But then her eyes widened as she glimpsed an extraordinary sight.

A great golden chariot drawn by strange winged creatures skimmed the treetops and landed in the clearing. Ravana swept Sita up in his arms and leapt into the chariot. She didn't even get a chance to scream before the chariot rose into the sky and flew away over the jungle.

"Rama, help!" Sita cried over and over. But it was no use. No one could hear. Sita was alone with the king of the Rakshas.

---

[12] A thatched roof is made of straw or grass.

Immediately Sita gathered her thoughts. She knew she would have to help herself. Looking down, she spotted a group of monkeys watching from the tops of some jungle trees. An idea formed in Sita's mind.

Carefully, so as not to attract Ravana's notice, Sita removed one of her golden bracelets. Its jewels glittered brightly in the sun. As the chariot passed over the monkeys, Sita threw the bracelet down to them. Ravana was too busy laughing over his victory to notice any of this.

As the chariot flew on, Sita dropped a jeweled necklace onto another group of monkeys. Later still, she tossed her earrings into the treetops.

Meanwhile, in the jungle, Lakshmana found Rama safe and alive.

"We've been tricked," Rama told his brother. "We've all been tricked. But where's Sita? Surely you didn't leave her alone?"

Before Lakshmana could even answer, the wilderness began to rumble with a low moaning sound. It sounded as if the beasts and birds, the insects and fishes, and even the trees themselves were in mourning.

Rama and Lakshmana knew something was very wrong. They rushed back to the bamboo house. "My wife is gone!" cried Rama.

The brothers wasted no time setting out to search for the missing princess. They traveled swiftly over the hills and streams and along the jungle paths. But Rama and Lakshmana found no sign of Sita at all.

On the second day of their search, Rama and Lakshmana came across a group of monkeys. Rama had learned the dangers of showing disrespect to others, so he spoke politely to the creatures.

"Kind monkeys, I wonder if you could help us?" asked Rama.

Sugriva,[13] the king of the monkeys, responded in kind. "What might we do for you, lords?"

---

[13] (soo grēv´ or soo grē´ va)

"Sita, my wife, is missing."

Rama then told the monkeys of their battle with the Rakshas and the episode of the magic deer.

"Those that battle against the Rakshas are friends of ours," Sugriva replied. "I will send word to all the monkeys in the jungle. If anyone can find clues to Sita's whereabouts, the monkeys will."

And sure enough, within a few hours, Sugriva brought Rama a collection of jewelry. Rama recognized every item as Sita's.

Sugriva nodded wisely. "The monkeys who found these things say they fell down from the sky," the monkey king said. "When the monkeys looked up, they saw a chariot carried through the air by winged beasts. I know of only one such chariot in all the world. It belongs to Ravana, king of the Rakshas."

Rama could not help but smile with pride. "The wise and gentle Sita has truly outsmarted Ravana," he declared.

"Indeed she has," agreed Lakshmana. "But where can Ravana have taken her?"

"To his kingdom, a place called Lanka," said Sugriva.

"And where can we find Lanka?" asked Rama.

"We've heard that it's across the great ocean to the south," Sugriva said.[14] "I will send for my most clever advisor, Hanuman.[15] If any of the monkeys can find the kingdom of the Rakshas, he can."

In a few minutes a wise-looking monkey stood before Rama and Sugriva. Hanuman agreed immediately to **conduct** the search for Sita.

"I would be honored to help," he said with sincerity.

Rama was overjoyed. "When you find Lanka, look for a woman with long black hair. She wears a jewel in the center of her forehead. If you find her, give her this ring. She will then know that I'm coming to her rescue."

Hanuman gathered a group of able monkeys and left for

---

[14] The ocean referred to is the Indian Ocean.
[15] (ha´ nu man)

the south. Before long they reached a large body of water. Hanuman caught a passing bird and asked it, "Is there land across this water?"

"Yes," said the bird. "But it's too far away for you to reach."

Hanuman laughed. Of all the monkeys in the world, he was the greatest jumper. He reared up and leapt out over the seemingly endless ocean. For hundreds of miles he soared above the water. At last, he neared a great island with a palace city on its coast.

Without a sound, Hanuman dropped inside the palace walls. In a courtyard, he saw a Raksha woman with wounds on her nose and ears.

"Surpa-Nakha!" he thought. "This is indeed the Raksha city. And I've surely found the palace of Ravana."

Hanuman scampered across the palace walls and roofs looking for Sita. He soon arrived at another courtyard which was guarded by fierce Raksha women. Inside he saw a human woman with long black hair and a jewel hanging on her forehead. She looked terribly **forlorn.** Hanuman tried to get her attention, but the woman never looked up.

Hanuman hurried down from the wall and played around the woman's feet, making chattering monkey sounds. She took no notice of the sounds at first. But soon she realized the monkey was speaking to her.

"I bring a message from your husband," Hanuman said. "He wants you to know that you will soon be rescued."

Sita stared at the creature in amazement. Then she looked into Hanuman's wise eyes and kindly face. She had no doubt that the monkey spoke the truth. She took his paw.

Hanuman gave her the ring Rama had sent. Sita quickly hid it in her robes. Relief and joy swept over her, but she sat quietly so the guards wouldn't notice. She removed the jewel from her own forehead and handed it to the monkey.

"Give this to my husband," she whispered. "Tell him I weep for him. Tell him that now I have hope."

Just then, Hanuman realized he had attracted the attention of the guards. He darted toward the palace walls, hoping to leap to freedom. But the guards set up a cry, and the monkey saw that he could not escape. He hid Sita's jewel in a wall just seconds before he was captured.

Hanuman was taken before Ravana, who was in terrible spirits. The Raksha king's eyes blazed with anger, for Sita would have nothing to do with him. The sight of the monkey didn't make him any happier. Ravana was well aware that monkeys could be **crafty** enemies.

"Kill the monkey at once," he told the guards.

The guards argued among themselves about the best way to kill Hanuman. Finally they tied an oily rag to the monkey's tail and set it on fire. Screaming wildly, the monkey scrambled to the top of a roof.

Hanuman's screams soon reached Sita's ears. She prayed desperately for this brave creature who had risked his life to bring her hope.

The gods heard Sita's prayers and saw to it that Hanuman was not harmed by the flames. Instead, as the monkey leapt from roof to roof of the city, house after house caught on fire. Before too long, much of the city was burning.

Hanuman found a pail of water and put out the fire on his tail. Then creeping through the smoke so nobody could see him, he found Sita's jewel. He grabbed it and escaped from the island.

The palace fire was soon put out. But Ravana was furious over the damage the flames had caused. And he knew that Rama would soon come to rescue his wife. Ravana held a meeting with his brothers to discuss his plans.

"First, I will kill the woman Sita," Ravana said to them. "She thinks herself too good for a Raksha king—she doesn't deserve to live. After Sita is dead, I'll defend Lanka against Rama and the monkeys."

But Vibhishana,[16] one of Ravana's brothers, objected. "It was wrong to kidnap this noble woman," he said. "I told you that from the beginning."

Another of Ravana's brothers, the giant Kumbha-karna,[17]

[16] (vib hē shan´ *or* vib hē sha´ na)
[17] (koomb´ karn *or* koom´ ba kar´ na)

woke up from his deep sleep long enough to voice his opinion. "I agree with Vibhishana," he said. "However, Ravana, you are our king. I will support your actions whether I agree with them or not."

With these words, Kumbha-karna dozed off again. The giant had a sleeping sickness that made it impossible for him to stay awake very long.

"Killing her and making war will only make a bad thing worse," Vibhishana insisted. "You must set things right by setting her free."

Ravana rose to his feet. "I'll never set her free!" he shouted fiercely. "You're a traitor and a coward. If you were not my brother, I would kill you as well. Either take my side or leave!"

Without another word, Vibhishana left the city. Ravana continued talking with his other brothers, who decided to stay and support the king. Together, they organized the fierce Raksha troops to defend Lanka against the coming threat.

Meanwhile, Hanuman reached home again, breathless from his terrible adventure. Rama was **elated** at the sight of Sita's jewel.

"She weeps for you," the monkey told Rama. "But she's grateful to have hope again."

Without further delay, Rama set about planning the attack on Lanka and Sita's rescue. Suddenly Lakshmana spied a Raksha coming toward them and immediately got ready to attack.

"Wait!" said the Raksha. "I come in peace. My name is Vibhishana. I'm here to tell you that you must march on the city at once. My brother Ravana plans to kill Sita. There's no time to be lost."

"But why are you telling us this?" asked Rama.

"I want to join you," said Vibhishana simply.

Following Rama's orders, the monkeys cut down thousands of trees and built a bridge to Lanka. Then an army of monkeys—led by Rama, Lakshmana, and Vibhishana—marched toward the Raksha kingdom in high spirits.

The Rakshas attacked Rama's army even before they

reached the island. The battle was long and fierce. The Rakshas changed into monsters and hurled magic at the attackers. But the monkeys were excellent warriors—swift and full of surprises.

Rama defeated most of Ravana's brothers with his powerful bow. Then he went after Kumbha-karna.

The giant brother of Ravana was barely able to wake himself for the battle. But he did his part for the Rakshas by devouring hundreds of monkeys. Finally Rama shot one arrow through Kumbha-karna's heart, killing the giant instantly.

At last, Rama broke through the palace wall and entered the courtyard where Ravana was holding Sita captive. Rama arrived just as Ravana was about to murder Sita.

"Come use your sword in a real challenge," called Rama. "You hide from battle to do your damage on a defenseless woman. Prepare to die."

"You'll be the one who dies, not I," was Ravana's reply.

Ravana swung his sword and nearly cut Rama with the sharp blade. Then Ravana tried to escape by changing into a bird.

Whispering prayers to the gods, Rama drew the bow of Vishnu and released an arrow. The Raksha king was struck dead in his tracks before he even knew what hit him.

Ravana's death put an end to the battle. The Raksha warriors quickly dropped their weapons and surrendered.

Though Ravana had done much evil, Rama treated the king's body with respect. He ordered a funeral pyre[18] built for Ravana. Vibhishana, now the king of Lanka, lit the pyre.

As the fire burned, the gentle Sita appeared. Joyfully and gracefully, she walked toward her husband.

Rama, too, was overjoyed to see his wife again. But he took care not to let others see his joy.

You see, Rama knew in his heart that Sita had been faithful to him. But he also knew that others would always doubt her **fidelity** if she were not tested. So he crossed his arms and pretended to be displeased with her.

---

[18] (pī er) A funeral pyre is a pile of wood used to burn a dead body.

Sita gazed deeply into Rama's eyes. She understood his thoughts. "Build another pyre for me, Lakshmana," she said simply.

Rama made no move to stop his brother. When the pyre was lighted, Sita turned to the crowd. "I swear that I have been faithful to my husband in every way," she said. "If I lie, let me die in this blaze!" And with those words, the brave princess stepped into the flames.

For a moment, Sita seemed to be swallowed up by the flames. The entire crowd gasped and cried aloud and wept. Still Rama stood with his arms folded, showing no emotion of any kind.

Suddenly, the flames of the pyre parted. Before the amazed eyes of the crowd, Sita walked out of the flames and stepped into her husband's grateful arms. She was not injured. Not a hair had been burned. Not even her clothing had been scorched.

"The gods knew what I myself knew," Rama shouted to the astonished crowd. "And now the world knows too. Sita never gave in to the evil Ravana—was never unfaithful to me. And now Brahma[19] himself has given her back to me."

With that, the happy couple and Lakshmana returned to their bamboo house in the jungle clearing. They remained there in peace until their exile was over. Almost before they knew it, it was time to return to the kingdom of Ayodhya.

The three arrived at the palace to a joyful welcome. Rama was delighted to see his people once again. But before he joined in the homecoming celebration, he had something to do.

Alone, Rama headed straight for his throne. He looked thoughtfully at the sandals Bharata had placed there so long ago. They had done a good job in his absence.

Stepping into the shoes, Rama said to himself, "The king of Ayodhya is now ready to rule in person!"

---

[19] (bra´ ma) Brahma is a major Hindu god. He is the creator of earthly life.

INSIGHTS

The story of Rama and Sita is just a small part of a larger collection of myths called the *Ramayana*. The *Ramayana* has roots in ancient Hindu mythology. The epic wasn't written down until sometime between 200 B.C. and 200 A.D. At that time a poet named Valmiki recorded it.

We know little about Valmiki except that he was a religious hermit. It is thought that he spent his life collecting stories about Rama. Then he put them together and shaped them into one long poem.

The poem was composed in Sanskrit, a language said to be older than Latin. Some people believed that Sarasvati, the wife of the god Brahma, invented the Sanskrit alphabet.

Dasa-ratha, Rama's father, was torn with grief at Rama's banishment. He was so grief-stricken, in fact, that he died. But in more than one way, the king had only himself to blame for his death.

As a young man, Dasa-ratha was filled with pride. His talents were so great that he forgot about being humble. This overconfidence ended up costing him dearly.

The king's mistake came when he was walking through the woods one day. He heard the sound of an elephant drinking from a stream. Without even looking, he pointed an arrow and shot it.

But the "elephant" turned out to be a young boy drawing water. The boy died, and a shaken Dasa-ratha went to tell the youth's mother and father.

The parents cursed Dasa-ratha. They told him that one of his own sons would be taken from him and that he would die of a broken heart. And as the couple predicted, so followed Rama's exile and the king's death.

continued

The ancient Indians believed that things moved in cycles. Like the changing seasons, all life—gods and humans included—moved from birth to death and back to birth again.

This belief was expressed in the idea of *reincarnation.* According to this concept, the souls of the dead return to earth in different bodies.

It is interesting to note that reincarnation plays a part in the Rama story. Rama was not only an earthly prince. He was also a reincarnation of the god Vishnu, who came to earth in order to kill the evil Ravana.

Ravana, too, was an incarnated god. At one time, he had a high position in Vishnu's heaven. Then he committed a serious error and was sentenced to three incarnations as Vishnu's enemy.

In this myth, we meet Ravana during his second return to earth. As the Raksha king, he gained a promise from the god Brahma that he would not be killed by a god or a demon. But foolish Ravana didn't bother to ask for protection from human beings. He felt himself too powerful to be overcome by them.

For this reason, Vishnu was reincarnated as the human Rama. Thus he was able to kill Ravana for the second time.

And in a way, Rama did Ravana a favor. Death meant the end of Ravana's second incarnation and left only one more to go.

What is the origin of Kumbha-karna's mysterious sleeping sickness?

It seems Kumbha-karna, a giant-monster, had such a huge appetite that he devoured everything in sight. The terrified people turned to the gods for help.

In response, the god Brahma gave Kumbha-karna the gift of eternal sleep. But the giant asked one favor. He wanted to be allowed to wake up once every six months to eat his fill. His wish was granted.

It is said that at one meal Kumbha-karna ate 6,000 cows, 10,000 sheep, 10,000 goats, and 400 buffalo. And he still complained of hunger!

The epic of Rama and Sita reads like an adventure story. But to the Hindus the myth also holds moral lessons. It provides a guide for living their lives.

The Hindus see Rama and Sita as examples of the perfect man and woman. Rama is an obedient son who respects the wishes of his father and the laws of his country. Sita is the ideal wife who remains faithful to her husband.

Rama's test of Sita near the end of the myth may seem cruel to us. But the Hindus understood and respected his actions. As king, Rama was an example to the citizens. If he accepted a wife who had been unfaithful, then that allowed everyone else to do the same.

Today the *Ramayana* remains important to Hindus. Every fall the epic is acted out by Indian citizens. The ritual lasts over a week and includes religious songs and dances.

LINDU'S VEIL OF STARS

VOCABULARY PREVIEW

Below is a list of words that appear in the story. Read the list and get to know the words before you read the story.

ascended—moved upward
clusters—groups; flocks
dejected—unhappy; low-spirited
dependable—trustworthy; responsible
destination—goal; journey's end
diversity—variety
fiancé—man engaged to be married
flared—blazed; burned
hue—color
inconstant—changeable; not dependable
predictable—regular; easy to foretell
routine—habit; regular actions
shimmered—glowed; shone
sphere—ball; globe
spontaneity—tendency to act on impulse or spur of the moment
stable—steady; worthy of trust
subjects—those ruled by a king or queen
suitor—admirer; one who romances another
trumpeted—announced noisily
wheeled—turned

Main Characters

Lindu—queen of the birds; daughter of Ukko
Northern Lights—one of Lindu's suitors
Ukko—king of heaven; Lindu's father

LINDU'S
VEIL OF STARS

A Finno-Ugric myth from Northern Europe

The lovely Lindu has begun to attract the attention of many admirers. At first she isn't interested. Then along comes a suitor as carefree as she is. But is he too carefree?

The geese arched their necks and paraded up and down the beach. Their cousins, the ducks, bobbed in the water of the Baltic Sea.[1] The smaller birds fluttered in circles and finally perched in the branches of nearby trees. They had all come to see the goddess Lindu[2]—Queen of the Birds.

"Here comes our queen," sang a nightingale. It flew up the beach to meet the young goddess.

"How beautiful she looks," quacked one of the ducks. "She is truly the daughter of Ukko,[3] the King of Heaven."

Lindu walked along the shore of the sea until she reached the **clusters** of birds. She wore a simple gown and sandals, but her shawl **shimmered** in the light. It was decorated with

---

[1] The Baltic Sea is a northern body of water surrounded by Sweden, Finland, Poland, Germany, Denmark, and the former Soviet Union.

[2] (lin´ doo)

[3] (oo´ kō)

brightly colored feathers the birds had given to her.

In the distance Lindu could see gray clouds. A chilly wind blew across the beach. The wind ruffled the feathers of the birds sitting in the trees. It made Lindu pull her shawl more tightly around her shoulders. Both she and the birds knew that winter was coming soon.

"As your queen, I am responsible for your well-being," Lindu said to the birds. "It is time for us to plan your journey to warmer lands. I will make sure you all travel safely and return to me in the spring."

Each group of birds came forward in its turn. The leaders told Lindu where the group had gone the previous winter. Lindu listened carefully to the leaders' reports. Then she told some of them to change their routes. She advised others to change their **destination.** Finally she was sure she had worked out the best possible plan for the coming winter.

"I shall miss you, my feathered friends," she said to them. "But it is better for you if you start your journeys soon."

In the following days, the head of each group of birds called its flock together. One by one, each great swarm rose and circled over the land. One by one, each group flew past Lindu and called, "Good-bye, our queen."

Finally the last flock set off for the south—toward warmer lands where they could survive the winter.

And so it went, year after year. Each fall, Lindu waved farewell to the birds. Each spring, they returned to their queen. Lindu was always overjoyed to see her **subjects** again. She helped them build their nests and raise their young through the long summer.

By now Lindu had become quite a radiant young woman. She started attracting the attention of numerous gods of the heavens. Many a handsome god spoke to Lindu's father, Ukko, King of the Heavens. Each one wanted Lindu for his wife. But Ukko said that Lindu must make her own choice of a husband.

The Sun was the first to ask Lindu to become his wife. The bright **sphere** waited until a cloudy and dreary day when he would be the most welcome.

The Sun found the Queen of the Birds sitting near the sea, huddling beneath her shawl. Suddenly he burst proudly through the clouds.

"Queen of the Birds," declared the Sun, "your subjects speak highly of you. They love you nearly as much as they love me. Become my wife and we will be the finest couple in the land."

Lindu smiled at the sun. She welcomed the warmth he had brought to the gloomy day. And he usually was very happy. But she shook her head.

"Warm and cheerful Sun," Lindu said politely, "you do me a great honor. But I'm afraid your life would be too boring for me. Every day you rise, cross the heavens, and set again. Why can't you change your **routine** from time to time?"

"But I do change my routine," said the Sun. He laughed and **flared** even more brightly. "At different times of the year, I rise earlier and set later. Sometimes I travel high into the sky. At other times, I stay closer to the earth. How can you say that my life is boring?"

"It's still the same old path day after day," Lindu answered. "It may seem exciting to you, but I'm used to more **diversity.**

"I wander on the shore, no matter whether it's day or night. I swim in the sea and climb in the trees. I sleep in the meadow grass whenever I please. I couldn't be happy with you. You're just too **predictable."**

So the Sun continued his path across the sky. He blazed more brightly than ever, but Lindu paid no attention to him.

The Moon was the next to propose to Lindu. He rose grandly over the water one night while Lindu walked alone on the beach. His silvery light reflected off the water at the queen's feet.

"Goddess," said the Moon, "you are almost as radiant as I am. The two of us would make a lovely couple. Become my wife, and we will be the envy of all who see us."

Lindu looked at the Moon thoughtfully. There was no doubt that he was handsome in his shining white robes. She especially liked the soft glow that he gave off wherever he went. But she did not want to marry the Moon.

"Beautiful Moon," Lindu said respectfully, "you do me a great honor. But I'm afraid that your life would be too boring for me. Every day you follow the same path through the heavens. Don't you get tired of the same old view?"

"My dear, you are mistaken," said the Moon. "Some days I rise earlier, some later. Sometimes I travel the sky during the light of day. Other times I come out at night—when I am most handsome. Why, I even change my shape and size! How can you say that my life is boring?"

"Still, your life lacks **spontaneity,**" Lindu answered. "Those small changes may seem exciting to you, but every day is different for me. One day I might explore a cave and play in the sand. The next I might watch as my new birds hatch and grow their feathers. I even help them learn to fly. I could not be happy with your routine life."

So the Moon went on his way and continued his nightly journey across the sky. He was especially large and bright that night. But Lindu wouldn't change her mind.

After a time the Pole Star[4] came to seek the hand of Lindu. He was a noble fellow and kind of heart. But Lindu knew that she could not bear to share the life of the Pole Star. Why, he was even more set in his ways than the Sun and the Moon! Every night, the Pole Star took up the same position. Then he watched as all the other stars **wheeled** busily around him.

Lindu turned the Pole Star down as kindly as she had the Sun and Moon. That night, he smiled down at her from his place in the northern sky. But Lindu wouldn't change her mind.

The next **suitor** for Lindu's hand was not like the others at all. The goddess met him while she was wandering on the beach early one morning. In fact, the world was still dark.

Suddenly a hint of gold showed in the northern sky, though it was too early for the dawn. Then more colors

---

[4] The Pole Star, or the North Star, is always located due north. It is actually two stars which appear to be one.

followed. Blue and red and every **hue** of the rainbow glowed brilliantly.

"Ah," Lindu said in wonder. "It is the Northern Lights.[5] How beautiful he is!"

The colors danced and swirled around the sky for hours. Finally they disappeared.

Lindu felt sad when the colors were gone. She had seen the Northern Lights before, but she could never tell when he would appear again. He came and went whenever he pleased, never following an exact schedule. And tonight he had been handsomer than ever before.

Lindu's feelings confused her. For reasons she couldn't understand, the goddess crept down to the beach every night. There she waited for the Northern Lights to reappear.

Just when it seemed he would never return, the Northern Lights delighted Lindu with a visit early one morning. Once again the dark sky was filled with a whirlwind of colors.

Then the Northern Lights spoke. "Lindu, daughter of Ukko," he said, "you are almost as free and wild as I am. The two of us could go on wonderful adventures together. Become my wife, and we will wander the heavens and the earth as we please."

Lindu looked at the Northern Lights and smiled. Suddenly she understood these new emotions stirring in her heart. She was in love with this beautiful suitor who danced in the sky.

"Northern Lights," Lindu said warmly, "you do me a great honor. And I realize you're the only one I can truly love. Yes, I will be your wife. We'll have a wonderful life together."

Lindu held her hands toward the sky. The Northern Lights glowed even more brightly. The dancing lights reached out and spun around Lindu's upraised hands. But by this time, the sun had started to rise.

"I cannot stay in the bright light of day for long," said the Northern Lights. "I will have to leave you for now."

---

[5] The northern lights, or aurora borealis, is a display of colors in the sky. It appears in the far north. The lights occur when particles from the sun strike the earth's magnetic field, creating electricity.

"When will you return?" asked Lindu.

"The moment it is dark, I shall come back. Then we'll celebrate our wedding and begin our life together," replied the Northern Lights.

After the glorious lights dimmed and disappeared, Lindu rushed to tell her subjects. The birds sang a joyful song when they heard the wonderful news. The geese flapped their mighty wings in the air and **trumpeted** their congratulations.

Then Lindu climbed to the top of the tallest hill and called to her father. Ukko, the King of Heaven, listened from his throne in the sky.

"Father, I have finally found someone who is just right for me," Lindu said. "I've agreed to marry the Northern Lights. He'll return tonight, and we'll be married."

Ukko was happy that his daughter had at last found someone she loved. But he was a little worried about her choice.

"Are you sure he is **dependable?"** Ukko asked.

"Of course he is," said Lindu. "He proposed to me. And he promised to return as soon as night falls. I'll have to hurry to get ready."

Lindu spent the day happily preparing for her wedding. Her birds all gave her plenty of help. They cleaned up a small clearing near the sea for the ceremony. Then they scattered flowers and their brightest and shiniest feathers on the grass. A few birds brought sweet-smelling herbs and scattered those around too. Soon the clearing was ready for the royal wedding.

Some of the other gods and goddesses came to help Lindu too. They quickly wove a fine white fabric and fashioned it into a gorgeous wedding dress. Then they knotted shining white threads into a long lace wedding veil.

Finally the goddesses dressed Lindu and combed her hair. When they placed the magnificent veil on her head, Lindu looked lovelier than ever before.

That night the Queen of the Birds stood in the clearing and waited for her **fiancé** to appear. The birds slept in the trees and on the ground around the clearing. They planned to wake up the moment the Northern Lights appeared. The gods and goddesses also waited patiently for the service to begin.

At midnight, the Northern Lights had still not arrived. The birds slept peacefully on, but the gods and goddesses grew restless. At dawn, the groom was still missing.

Lindu was very disappointed. But she put on a brave face and said, "Don't worry. He'll come."

The next night, Lindu and the birds and the gods and goddesses again gathered in the clearing. And again the Northern Lights did not show up. This time, Lindu grew even sadder, and the gods and goddesses grew impatient.

"That Northern Lights just isn't dependable," one of the gods said. "You should have chosen someone more **stable.**"

"He's **inconstant,**" a goddess murmured. "He never appears when you want him to, even if he promised."

Lindu waited in the clearing for three more nights, but the Northern Lights never showed himself. Each evening Lindu's loyal birds gathered there with her. But the gods and goddesses had all given up and gone home. Only Ukko sadly watched from his throne in the Heavens. His daughter's increasing unhappiness tore at his heart.

As the morning of the sixth day dawned, Lindu looked around the clearing. The flowers had all wilted. The bright feathers had been trampled underfoot. The sweet smell of the herbs had blown away with the breeze.

The **dejected** goddess looked down at her dress. The lovely white gown was damp with her tears. Lindu sat on a stone in the clearing and began to weep again.

The birds fluttered around Lindu and tried to cheer her up. But their songs did not stop the goddess from shedding tears.

"He was the only one exciting enough for me to love," she wept.

"Please don't cry, our Queen," cooed the nightingale. "You're not alone. You still have all your loyal subjects. We love you."

"But you must go south very soon," wept Lindu. "And then I'll be left here all by myself. How can I bear that?"

Lindu's words caused great concern among the birds.

They chirped and quacked and honked to each other. Then they gathered back around Lindu.

"We will not go south this fall," quacked the leader of the ducks. "We won't leave you here all alone. We'll stay with you until you feel better."

The other birds agreed. They all chirped and sang and honked their decision to stay with their Queen until she felt better.

"No, no, my devoted subjects," Lindu said with a sigh. "If you stay here, you'll all die. You don't know how terrible the winter is. I would be truly miserable if my subjects froze to death in the snow."

The birds strutted and flapped in confusion. They didn't know what to do. Most simply kept promising never to leave their queen alone in her misery. But Lindu continued to shake her head sadly.

Ukko, King of the Heavens, took pity on his daughter. He knew it would be useless to try to force the Northern Lights to marry Lindu. The flashy suitor might go through with the wedding, but he would soon wander off again. Lindu would never be happy if she was married to a husband who disappeared whenever he pleased.

Ukko also knew that those birds who refused to leave their grieving queen would certainly die. So Ukko decided on a different solution to the problem.

"Come, daughter," Ukko said. "Join me here in the heavens."

"Father, I would love to live there near you," Lindu answered. "But who would take care of my birds? Who would see that they all migrate to the right places every fall?"

"From here you can easily oversee their journeys," said Ukko.

Lindu thought for a while. Then she smiled for the first time in days. She nodded happily and reached up toward her father. The birds chirped, sang, quacked, and honked their approval.

Ukko commanded the wind to bring his daughter to him, and Lindu **ascended** into the heavens. She was lifted higher than the Northern Lights could ever go—higher than the Moon and higher than the Sun. She rose above the Pole Star into the uppermost heavens where her father lived.

As she was raised into the heavens, Lindu looked behind her. Her long lace wedding veil trailed behind and spread across the sky. The threads of the veil were turned into a million stars which sparkled in the heavens.

Today Lindu's veil can still be seen in the sky at night. The stars from her veil form the band of light we call the Milky Way.[6]

Lindu loves being in the heavens where she can see and enjoy more worlds than she ever imagined existed. And she continues to take care of her beloved birds. She arranges their routes and watches over their journeys as they fly from north to south and back again.

From time to time, Lindu sees the dancing colors of the Northern Lights. But from her place in the heavens, she doesn't find him as charming as before. And she now understands that he is truly undependable. Someone like that could never help take care of her birds. He would never be there when needed.

"What did I ever see in him?" Lindu wonders. Then she puts him out of her mind as she watches a brand new star appear and sparkle in her long veil.

[6] The Milky Way is made up of stars in our own galaxy.

INSIGHTS

Lindu's Veil of Stars" is a myth from the Finno-Ugric culture. The ancient Finno-Ugric people were hunters who wandered throughout northern Europe and Russia. They settled in such places as Finland, Siberia, Russia, and Estonia. Today the far-flung groups are still related because they speak versions of the same language.

In ancient times, singers roamed throughout the region relating the legends and folktales of the people. To accompany their singing, they often played a type of harp called a *kantele*.

In the 19th century, a man named Elias Lonnrot collected and wrote down many of these songs. He called the collection the *Kalevala*—a name which roughly translates as "Land of Heroes."

Though the story of Lindu is not included in this work, her father Ukko is mentioned several times.

Ukko stands out among the Finno-Ugric deities. He is the supreme god and also the god of thunder.

It is said that Ukko invented fire when his sword struck his fingernail, causing a small flame. This flame was accidentally dropped into a lake on earth. A passing fish promptly snapped it up, and for a while it seemed that humans would never see fire.

But then the Finnish hero Vainamoinen—the inventor of music and poetry—caught the fish and set the fire free.

Maan-Eno, Ukko's wife, is another honored deity. She is important because she oversees the success of the harvest.

Also important to some Finno-Ugric peoples were household spirits. These spirits took the form of men and supposedly lived under the floor.

A household spirit—sometimes called "house man"—protected the occupants from harm. He was also helpful. Sometimes at night he would complete chores that were left undone during the day.

The religion of most Finno-Ugric people is tied closely to the natural world. These people believe that spirits dwell in all beings and objects. They also believe that the soul clings to the skeleton.

In fact, some Finno-Ugric people feel that without a skeleton, there is no soul. For this reason, these people refuse to break or destroy the bones of a sacrificed animal. They believe that the gods use the skeleton—and the soul within it—to create another animal.

Today, many descendants of the Finno-Ugric culture still hold to their ancient beliefs.

Bodies of dead people are also carefully taken care of. For as long as the body is not decayed, the soul is very much alive.

Some tribes believe that corpses can rise at night. Sometimes the bodies even try to start fights with living people. Their solution—before burial, corpses are pinned to the ground with a stake.

Lindu wasn't the only one to think that the North Star was set in his ways. Many Finno-Ugric tribes at one time believed that the North Star supported the heavens. The heavens, along with all the other stars, revolved around it.

Some Finno-Ugric tribes called the North Star the "nail of the sky." It was believed by some that one day an archer would shoot down the North Star with his arrow. Then the heavens would fall to earth, and the world would be ended.

BAO CHU'S SEARCH FOR THE SUN

VOCABULARY PREVIEW

Below is a list of words that appear in the story. Read the list and get to know the words before you read the story.

brandished—displayed; waved
braving—facing; confronting
cowered—crouched in fear
demons—devils; evil spirits
forked—split; divided
frantic—wild; out-of-control
ghastly—frightful; hideous
gratitude—thankfulness; appreciation
heaved—lifted; carried up
prospered—grew well; increased
protested—objected; argued
quest—look; search
slinging—throwing, usually with a swinging motion
sturdy—solidly built; strong
thicket—thick growth of shrubs or small trees
torment—trouble; torture
transform—change; alter
traversing—traveling over; crossing
(in) vain—for nothing
withered—shriveled; dried out

Main Characters

Bao Chu—son of Hui Niang and Liu Chun
Hui Niang—wife of Liu Chun; mother of Bao Chu
Liu Chun—simple farmer; husband of Hui Niang; father of Bao Chu

BAO CHU'S SEARCH
FOR THE SUN

A myth from China

*What are the people of Gemstone Mountain to do?
The sun has mysteriously disappeared, leaving
crops to die. And in the shadows, fearful demons
now stalk. The people's only hope rests with a
courageous son and his strong-hearted mother.*

The people who lived in the small village at the foot of Gemstone Mountain were peaceful and happy. Their village was on the shore of West Lake, which provided them with fish to eat. The villagers also grew lovely gardens of food and flowers, and their chickens and cows were fat and healthy. Every day the sun warmed their gardens, and rain fell when it was needed.

The people of the village admired those who worked hard, used good common sense, and took care of their families. The villagers honored their elders because they knew great wisdom came with age. Everything went well in the village.

Then one day, just after the sun rose in the east, a terrible disaster struck. The most violent rainstorm anyone had ever seen blew across the village. Black clouds hid the sun from view. Through the mist and clouds, the villagers could see the light of day growing dim. It looked as though the sun had gone down again, exactly where it had just come up.

When the clouds cleared, the villagers gathered together and looked toward the east. But there was no sun to be seen. Anxiously they waited, but the sun didn't reappear. They spoke to each other in whispers.

"Surely the sun will come up again in just a few moments," said a **sturdy** farmer.

"What could have happened?" asked a young man. "Where is the sun?"

"The sun has come up every day for as long as anyone can remember," said an old woman.

The villagers watched and waited. But there was no sign of the sun. After a while, everybody went home. Days and days went by—or what *should* have been days. In fact, there was only night.

As this cold night grew longer, plants **withered.** The crops in the fields began to die, and trees lost their leaves.

To make matters worse, **demons** and ghosts—evil creatures who hated the light and loved the dark—roamed the land at will.

Again the people gathered in order to decide what to do.

"All of our crops are dying. And it will do no good to plant more," one farmer said.

"The chickens are laying no eggs," said an old woman.

"The animals can find nothing to eat," said a young man. "They are growing thin and will soon die."

"The fish are not biting," said a fisherman. "Even if they did, we could not go out on the water. The world is now filled with demons who capture and **torment** our people."

In this unfortunate village lived a farmer named Liu Chun.[1] His wife, Hui Niang,[2] was a weaver. This young couple was much admired because they worked hard and were very sensible.

Liu Chun decided he had to do something about the terrible situation. He went to see the oldest person in the village—a man of 180 years.

"Can you tell me what's wrong?" Liu Chun asked. "What could have become of our sun?"

"I believe that I know what happened," the elder answered. "Someone who hates the sun has taken it away."

[1] (lē´u chung)
[2] (hoo´ē nē ang´)

"But honored sir, who could hate the sun?" Liu Chun **protested** gently. "Humans and animals all suffer terribly from this constant darkness."

"Think for a moment, young farmer," said the old man. "Who benefits from this long night?"

Liu Chun thought for a moment. He answered, "The demons now roam the world at will and do as they please. Only they are happy for the sun to be gone."

"Quite true," said the old man. "The ghosts and demons love the darkness because it hides their evil deeds. The sun is their enemy."

"I didn't know that those creatures had the power to destroy the sun," Liu Chun said.

"No, even they could not destroy it," explained the elder. "There is a demon king who rules over all evil creatures. I believe that he has stolen the sun and hidden it away. He is the only one who could do such a thing."

"Where is this demon king?" asked Liu Chun.

"He lives beneath the Eastern Sea," the elder replied.

Liu Chun thanked the elder for his help. Then he went home and told his wife that he was going to find the sun.

"I must do something," Liu Chun said. "The people are suffering and I cannot bear their pain. The elder has given me a clue where to look."

"I'll help you in any way that I can," answered Hui Niang.

So Hui Niang made her husband a warm new coat. She wove two strong layers and stitched thick cotton inside. She also took some of her own long hair and twisted it together with strands of hemp.[3] Hui Niang then worked the strands into a new pair of sandals for Liu Chun.

When Liu Chun was ready to leave, Hui Niang stood outside to wave good-bye to her husband. Suddenly a bright golden light shone in the sky. For a moment, the couple thought that the sun had returned.

But this light moved rapidly toward them. They could see

---

[3] Hemp is a plant used to make rope.

that it was small, and they could feel that it did not give off heat.

The bright light flew right up to Liu Chun. When it landed on his shoulder, they saw that it was a golden bird.

"A phoenix!"[4] exclaimed Hui Niang. "Surely this wonderful creature has come to help you."

Liu Chun asked the phoenix, "Will you join me on my journey?"

The phoenix bent its long, graceful neck and nodded its head.

"I will go now," Liu Chun said to his wife. "The golden phoenix will light my way in this endless night. I won't return until I've found the sun.

"If I should be killed," continued Liu Chun, "I will turn myself into a bright star in the sky. From there I will guide others who **quest** for the sun."

With the golden phoenix glowing on his shoulder, Liu Chun set off into the dark.

Meanwhile, Hui Niang stayed behind and waited, **braving** demons and ghosts with the rest of the villagers. Every day she climbed to the top of Gemstone Mountain and peered into the East. She waited patiently for signs of the sun.

One day Hui Niang thought she saw a light in the east. But it was not the sun. Instead she saw a bright new star rising into the sky. Then she saw a smaller light moving toward her. As the light grew larger, she saw it was the phoenix.

"Why isn't my husband with you?" asked Hui Niang after the golden bird landed at her feet. "Where is Liu Chun?"

The phoenix hung its little head as if in sorrow.

Hui Niang now knew the terrible truth. Her husband was dead. Grief flooded over her, and she fainted away on the mountaintop.

At that moment, Hui Niang might have been carried away by the demons. But the phoenix stood near her. The bird's golden glow protected the grief-stricken widow.

---

[4] (fē´ nix) The phoenix is a mythical bird. It is known for its ability to live for hundreds of years and for its magical powers of rebirth.

Finally Hui Niang awoke. She discovered with surprise that she had given birth to a son.

Hui Niang looked with **gratitude** at the phoenix, who still stood nearby. "You have kept my son safe for me," she said to the bird. "Thank you."

Then she looked back at the child. "Bao Chu[5] shall be your name," she said. "I only wish your father could have lived to see you."

Then Hui Niang gathered up her child and prepared to climb back down the mountain. As they descended, a strong wind began to blow.

The wind did a remarkable thing. As the first gust blew across the baby's face, he began to speak. After the second gust, the child stood up and began to walk.

The third gust of wind spun the mother and child around. Hui Niang lost sight of her son and in fear called out to him.

"Bao Chu, where are you?"

"I am here," came a voice from above her head.

Hui Niang was surprised to see that her son had magically grown to be eighteen feet tall.

All the while, the phoenix had been watching from the branch of a nearby tree. As if in approval, the bird nodded. With a flutter of its wings, it flew away into the darkness.

When the light of the phoenix had disappeared, Hui Niang began the climb back down Gemstone Mountain. But before she'd gone four steps, her tall, strong son picked her up. Gently he carried his mother over the difficult places. So Hui Niang returned with Bao Chu to their little farmhouse.

Hui Niang was delighted with her new son. Even though Bao Chu was a bit large for the house and furniture, he was quiet and gentle. All the people of the village came to admire the giant boy who had been born to Hui Niang.

One day Bao Chu found his mother crying.

"Mother, why are you crying?" the boy asked. "Have I angered you in some way?"

"Oh no, Bao Chu," Hui Niang answered tearfully. "You

[5] (bow choo)

are a wonderful son. It's only that I wish you could have known your father. Liu Chun was a fine man, and I miss him very much."

"Where is my father?" Bao Chu asked.

"He was killed before you were born," Hui Niang said. She told him about the journey Liu Chun had made to try to find the sun. Then she pointed to the brightest star in the sky.

"You see, there is your father," Hui Niang said. "He told me that he would **transform** himself into a bright star. Your father shines in the sky to mark the way for anyone else who journeys to rescue the sun. But no other villager has been brave enough to follow him into the dark."

"So my father's mission goes unfinished," Bao Chu said. "With your permission, Mother, I will complete the task he started. I will follow the path my father marks with his starlight. I will find the sun."

Hui Niang didn't know what to do. Bao Chu would greatly honor his father by completing the quest. But Hui Niang also knew that she might lose Bao Chu. The demons in the darkness were truly ferocious. The demon king had to be even more terrible.

On the other hand, the villagers were suffering terribly from the cold and dark. They would all surely die if someone didn't find the sun and return it to the sky.

"My heart will ache if you leave," Hui Niang told her son. "But you are our only hope. Go, then, and may you find success."

Hui Niang made a warm coat and sandals for Bao Chu. The sandals and the coat were just like those she had made for Liu Chun. Of course, they had to be made much larger to fit Bao Chu.

Finally Bao Chu was ready to leave. As he was saying farewell, the phoenix appeared through the darkness and landed on his shoulder. The boy laughed with delight at the beauty of the glowing bird.

"The phoenix is your friend," said Hui Niang. "He joined your father on his quest. He will join you on your own journey, if you wish."

Bao Chu asked the phoenix, "Will you join me?"

The phoenix bent its long, graceful neck and nodded its head.

"Remember that your father marks the path you must take to find the sun," said Hui Niang.

Once again, she pointed out the brightest star in the sky to Bao Chu. Then Hui Niang put her hands up to her face and looked as though she might cry.

"Don't grieve for me, Mother," Bao Chu said. "No matter how long I'm gone, keep up your faith and don't cry. If you shed tears for me, it will break my heart. With a broken heart, I will weaken and will not be able to complete my father's quest."

Hui Niang nodded and promised not to cry for her son. Then the boy cheerfully waved good-bye and disappeared into the dark and endless night.

Bao Chu made his way up and down many hills and ravines. He often unexpectedly found himself at the edge of a sharp drop. If not for the phoenix's glow, Bao Chu would certainly have stumbled and fallen to his death.

As Bao Chu came down one mountain, he found himself in the middle of a **thicket** of thorn bushes. These were evil plants that had **prospered** in the land since the sun's disappearance. They actually reached out and grasped at Bao Chu as he made his way among them.

Fortunately, Bao Chu was wearing the new padded coat Hui Niang had made for him. Otherwise, he would surely have been badly slashed and might have bled to death there on the mountainside.

As things turned out, Bao Chu's coat became shredded, and he suffered many wounds. But at last he reached a small village at the foot of the mountain. He was greeted by the villagers, who eagerly gathered to see this young giant who had appeared out of the dark.

Bao Chu waited politely to speak until one of the village elders asked his name.

"I am Bao Chu," he said. "I've come to complete the quest of my father, Liu Chun. I want to find the sun and return it to the sky.

"But as you can see, the thorn bushes have torn my new coat to shreds," continued Bao Chu. "I'm very cold from the night and very sore from the attacks of the thorns."

"Young man, come into our village, and our people will care for you," the elder said.

The people of the village tended Bao Chu's wounds. They shared with him what little they had to eat. But they saw that they would not be able to repair the coat Hui Niang had made.

"We don't have much to offer you," said an old woman of the village. "Our plants and animals have died. But each of us can give a small square from our own clothing. From all of those squares, we will make you a new coat."

So all the people in the village tore small squares from their clothing. The women sewed the pieces together and made a new coat for Bao Chu. They called it their "Hundred Family Coat."

When Bao Chu was rested, he put on his new coat and thanked the villagers. Then, with the golden phoenix on his shoulder, he walked into the darkness and continued his quest.

Man and bird crossed many more mountains, avoiding the thickets of thorns. The boy's new coat kept him warm and comfortable.

As he continued on his journey, Bao Chu had to swim across many rivers. But one day he came to a river much wider than any of the others. Looking across the water, Bao Chu saw fierce rapids[6] topped with white waves. The raging river washed over sharp rocks and boulders.

Bao Chu looked up at the sky. The bright star was still directly ahead of them. "One way or another, we'll have to cross this river," Bao Chu said to the phoenix.

With these words, Bao Chu stepped boldly into the swift water. The current nearly knocked him down, and whirlpools threatened to drag him under. Bao Chu started swimming for his life.

---

[6] Rapids are fast-moving parts of a river.

Suddenly a wind swept across the river—the coldest wind the world had ever felt. Water snapped and crackled. Within a few minutes, the entire river was frozen solid. Bao Chu and the phoenix couldn't move.

Luckily, the Hundred Family Coat protected the boy from the freezing ice. The coat's warmth came from more than its fabric. It came from the caring and concern of the people in the village. Little by little, the coat's warmth began to melt some of the ice from around Bao Chu's body.

Bao Chu tucked the phoenix inside the coat. He felt the bird stir slightly, so he knew it was not dead. With one arm, Bao Chu held the bird tightly against him. Then with the other, he smashed his fist down against the ice. Again and again Bao Chu pounded the frozen stream.

Suddenly there came a loud cracking noise. The sound repeated and echoed all around Bao Chu in the dark night. He raised his arm and struck the ice again. With a mighty groan, the ice split into large chunks. The river started to move again.

Still holding onto the phoenix, Bao Chu scrambled to get up onto one of the ice floes.[7] Bao Chu then leapt from one ice floe to the next until he reached the far shore of the river.

Bao Chu immediately took the phoenix out from under his coat. The bird's golden feathers drooped, and its glow was very dim.

"Will the bird survive?" wondered Bao Chu. "I would soon be lost without the phoenix's light."

Bao Chu put the phoenix inside his coat and continued on his way. After a time, he reached another village.

Again, Bao Chu waited politely to speak until one of the village elders asked his name.

"My name is Bao Chu," he said. "I am seeking to find the sun and return it to the sky. But I nearly froze to death in a great river, and I'm very cold and tired."

These villagers, like the others, took Bao Chu in and warmed him. They gave the phoenix a dry place by a fire, and

---

[7] Floes are sheets of floating ice.

the bird soon began to glow brightly again.

These people had even less to eat than the people in the first village. But they shared what they had.

When Bao Chu had eaten, he said, "Thank you very much for your wonderful food. Now it's time for me to continue on my journey."

Before Bao Chu left, the oldest man of the village spoke to him. "We don't have much to offer you," the elder said. "Our plants and our animals have died. The most valuable thing we have is our soil. We have worked it all our lives, as our ancestors did before us. Perhaps it will be useful to you."

Each of the villagers put a handful of soil from their garden into a large bag. Bao Chu put the bag of soil on one shoulder and thanked the villagers. Then with the golden phoenix on his other shoulder, he walked into the darkness and continued his quest.

After climbing more mountains and crossing more rivers, Bao Chu came to a road that **forked.** One road appeared to go slightly to the left of the bright star that marked his way. The other road appeared to go slightly to its right. In between the roads, the country was too rough and thorny for anyone to pass.

Bao Chu stopped at the crossroads. As he stood and wondered which way to go, he heard footsteps behind him. He turned around and saw a small dark figure approaching him. When the figure came closer, he could see that it was an old woman.

Suddenly the phoenix rose up on Bao Chu's shoulder and flapped its wings angrily. Embarrassed at the bird's behavior, Bao Chu pushed it away from his shoulder. Of course, he waited politely to be greeted.

"Who are you, young man?" the old woman asked. "Where are you going out here in the endless night?"

"My name is Bao Chu," he said. "I've come to complete the quest of my father, Liu Chun. I want to find the sun and return it to the sky. But I have climbed many mountains and crossed many rivers, and I am growing very tired."

While they talked, the phoenix flew in **frantic** circles just above their heads. Both Bao Chu and the old woman tried to ignore the bird.

"It's much too long a journey," said the old woman. "You must return to your home. I'm sure your mother weeps for you."

"My mother has promised not to weep for me," Bao Chu answered. "And I will not return home until I have found the sun and returned it to the sky."

"Young people will never listen to those who are wiser," the old woman said with a sigh. "Well, if you must go on, take the road on the right."

As soon as the old woman said these words, the phoenix began to dive at her. The bird clawed at her face and struck her with its beak and its wide wings.

Bao Chu was furious. "What's the matter with you?" he yelled at the phoenix. "This woman is trying to help me!"

Bao Chu chased the golden bird away. Then he picked up a rock to throw if the phoenix attacked again.

The old woman continued giving Bao Chu advice. "If you go down the road to the right, you'll find the sun," she said. "But you'll come to a village before that, and I suggest that you rest there."

"Thank you for your kind advice," Bao Chu said. "I will follow it."

"Why don't you leave that bag of dirt here on the side of the road?" the old woman suggested. "It's silly to carry such a useless burden. It must be growing heavy."

Bao Chu smiled and said, "You're right. It's a heavy and useless bag of dirt. But it was a gift to me from many kind people. I can't leave it by the side of the road."

The old woman merely grumbled and frowned. Bao Chu put the bag of soil on his shoulder and started down the road to the right. After a few steps, he thought perhaps he should say good-bye to the old woman more politely. He turned around to speak to her, but she was gone.

Bao Chu shrugged and continued down the road. As he walked along, the phoenix flew in front of him and tried to block his way. Bao Chu had to threaten the bird with the rock before it would leave him alone.

"I wonder what's troubling the phoenix?" thought Bao Chu to himself. "I've never seen the bird attack anyone before, much less an elder."

The bird circled over Bao Chu's head, but it no longer tried to stop him.

Bao Chu had no difficulty **traversing** the road, even without the phoenix's light. The way was so smooth that he reached the village quite easily.

As Bao Chu walked into the village, the townspeople came out to greet him. They seemed already to know about his mission. And they praised his bravery and called him a hero. The people even began to arrange a feast to celebrate his arrival.

Although the sky was as dark here as everywhere else, this village seemed to be doing very well. The houses were well lit and the people well fed. The villagers were all dressed in fine clothing. Bao Chu watched them as they scurried around, cheerfully preparing his feast.

"How can these people be so rich and prosperous?" he wondered. "Everyone else I've seen has suffered terribly from the cold and the dark. Here the food is plentiful, and the people are healthy and happy."

As Bao Chu asked himself these questions, the village elder handed him a large wooden cup of wine. All the villagers raised their cups for a toast in his honor.

As Bao Chu raised his cup, something fell into it. Wine splashed into Bao Chu's face. Looking up, he saw the phoenix circling above him. Apparently the bird had dropped something into the cup.

Suddenly the object in Bao Chu's cup burst into flames. But before it turned to ashes, Bao Chu got a good look at it. It was a sandal made of hemp and hair twisted together—just like the ones he wore, only smaller.

"This looks like one of the sandals my mother made!" Bao Chu whispered to himself.

Then he shouted at the villagers, "This must be the place where my father died! Evil people! I knew something was wrong from the moment I arrived."

At the sound of Bao Chu's fury, all the houses of the village disappeared. The people vanished as well. In the surrounding darkness, only demons and ghosts **cowered** before Bao Chu. One by one the evil creatures slithered away into the darkness.

Bao Chu looked up and saw the phoenix still circling overhead. He felt ashamed of the way he had treated the loyal bird.

"You saved me from the demon village," Bao Chu called. "Please forgive me and become my companion once again."

To Bao Chu's relief, the golden phoenix circled downward and landed on his shoulder again. **Slinging** the bag of soil over his other shoulder, Bao Chu went back to the crossroads. This time, he took the road to the left.

The demons and ghosts now followed Bao Chu through the hills, moaning and muttering in anger. They hadn't been able to tear Bao Chu apart with their thorn bushes. They hadn't been able to freeze him with their cold wind. And they had failed to kill him in their village.

Now the mighty demons threw high mountains in Bao Chu's path. But Bao Chu had climbed many other mountains, so he made his way over these too. Then the ghosts placed swift rivers in his path. But Bao Chu had crossed many other rivers, and he swam across these too. In spite of everything the evil spirits did, the young hero continued in the direction of the brightest star.

As if in despair, the demons began to moan. The moan grew louder until it became an evil wind that wailed over the land.

The wind blew all the way back to Bao Chu's village at the foot of Gemstone Mountain. It blew through the village until it found the farmhouse of Bao Chu's mother. Then the demon wind moaned and whispered into Hui Niang's ear.

"Bao Chu slipped and fell from a steep cliff," the demons said to Hui Niang. "Bao Chu fell into the rocky river below. He was crushed to death in the fall. Your son, Bao Chu, is dead."

Over and over again the ghosts hissed, "Your son is dead, Hui Niang. Bao Chu is dead."

The demons and ghosts hoped that Hui Niang would be stricken with grief and weep for Bao Chu. They hoped that her tears would weaken the hero as he pursued his quest.

But Hui Niang remembered what Bao Chu had said: "If you shed tears for me, it will break my heart. With a broken heart, I will weaken and will not be able to complete my father's quest."

So Hui Niang fought back her tears and held her head high. "I don't believe you!" she yelled to the wind. "I refuse to listen to your whispering lies. I refuse to cry for Bao Chu."

The demons and ghosts had failed again. In fact, instead of discouraging Hui Niang, the demon wind brought her new hope. "The demons wouldn't try to trick me if Bao Chu were already dead," she said to herself.

Hui Niang and the villagers continued to keep watch faithfully. Every morning when it should have been dawn, they gathered large flat rocks and carried them up Gemstone Mountain. At the top, they put their rocks down and stood on them. They looked to the east in hope of seeing the sun.

Every day, each person piled a new rock on top of an older one. The rock wall on top of the mountain grew higher and higher. But the villagers who stood on the rocks still saw no sign of the sun.

Meanwhile, Bao Chu made his way in the direction of the brightest star in the sky. However, he was beginning to believe that his journey was as endless as the dark night. One mountain led to another mountain, and one river was replaced by another river.

Then, from the top of a high peak, Bao Chu heard an unfamiliar sound. A low repeated roar echoed in the distance.

"I believe I hear the sea," Bao Chu said to the phoenix.

The bird rose into the air and sped in the direction of the roar. After a short time, Bao Chu saw the golden light returning. The phoenix landed on his shoulder and nodded its graceful head.

Bao Chu went down the mountain and went on until he

found the shore of the Eastern Sea. The brightest star was straight ahead of him, reflected many times in the waves.

"Where can I go now?" Bao Chu wondered, looking at the broad, deep water. "The sea is much too wide for me to swim across."

Then Bao Chu remembered the bag of soil on his shoulder. It had been given to him by people who had nothing else to give.

"This soil must have been given to me for a reason," Bao Chu thought. "Maybe now is the time to try it out."

Bao Chu opened up the bag and poured all of the soil into the sea. For a moment, it just floated on the surface of the water.

Then as if by magic, a strong wind rose and blew across the waves. The wind scattered the soil over the water, pushing some of it together and pulling some of it apart. Soon the soil had been shaped into a series of islands which reached far out into the sea.

"What wonderful islands," Bao Chu said. "They're close enough together for me to swim from one to another."

And that is just what he did. With the phoenix still on his shoulder, Bao Chu swam to the first island. Then he rested for a few moments and swam to the next. He continued until he reached the last island.

There Bao Chu stood looking out to sea and wondering what to do next. But before he had time to form a plan, the island began to sink. Straight to the bottom of the sea went Bao Chu and the golden bird. To Bao Chu's amazement, he and the phoenix were easily able to breathe under the water.

By the light of the golden phoenix, Bao Chu saw an underwater cave yawning in front of him. Its opening was blocked with a huge boulder. But around the edges of the boulder, Bao Chu could see a glimmering light.

"That must be the light of the sun!" he cried. "The bright star has led us to exactly the right place. The demon king has trapped the sun in that cave!"

At that moment, an army of terrible monsters appeared in front of the cave. They all **brandished** sharp weapons and solid shields.

But Bao Chu paid no attention to them. Instead he looked at the leader of the **ghastly** army. He was the most horrible monster of all, and he carried a huge sword. "That must be the demon king," Bao Chu thought.

"If I kill that one," Bao Chu said to the phoenix, "the others will disappear."

The phoenix left the young hero's shoulder and swam near him in the sea. Though Bao Chu had no weapon, he bravely charged toward the demon king.

The king let loose an unearthly scream and swung his blade. But Bao Chu was swift and strong. He took hold of the demon king's shield and tore it from his hands. Then Bao Chu swung the shield and knocked the king's sword away too.

Then the two began to wrestle. They spun and jumped and struck out with their feet and fists. They rolled across the ocean floor.

After a time, Bao Chu grew weak from his many wounds. But he wasn't ready to give up. He summoned his strength and spun around one more time. He landed a mighty blow in demon king's stomach.

The evil king stumbled and fell. A deep growl rose from the ranks of the watching army. Just as they were about to rush forward to defend their king, the swimming phoenix darted into the battle. The golden bird swiftly tore out the demon king's eyes with his beak.

The demon king thrashed around blindly. In his rage, he bumped into a mountain of boulders. The huge stones tumbled down on top of him, crushing out his life.

With the death of their king, the army of demons disappeared completely. Bao Chu fell to the ocean floor in exhaustion.

"But I haven't finished yet," Bao Chu reminded himself. Wearily, he got to his feet and went to the cave. He strained against the boulder that blocked the entrance. Little by little, Bao Chu moved the boulder aside. Finally, the light of the sun fell upon him.

With the last of his strength, Bao Chu took the huge sun in

his arms and swam toward the surface of the sea. The phoenix swam alongside him. Bao Chu kicked harder and harder, trying to reach the surface before weakness overcame him.

"I can't stop now," he told himself over and over. "I'm too close to fulfilling my mission to quit."

At last Bao Chu reached the top. Straining, he **heaved** the sun out of the water just before his strength gave out.

Bao Chu knew he could do no more. "You must finish this for me," he told the phoenix weakly. "You must return the sun to the sky so my father will not have died in **vain."** Then Bao Chu closed his eyes for the last time.

The golden phoenix dived beneath the sun. It spread its wings and lifted the globe until it was out of the water.

Freed now, the sun rose gloriously into the air. After so many days of darkness, it again spread its brightness over the earth.

A hideous moan began as demons and ghosts were caught in the sun's light. Those that failed to find shelter from the sun immediately turned to stone.

At that moment, Hui Niang and the villagers were on Gemstone Mountain looking toward the east. They were all standing on the high piles of stones they'd raised.

"Look! There's a purple glow on the eastern horizon," said one villager.

"I don't see anything," said another. "You've been watching so long that you're seeing things."

"No, look!" cried Hui Niang. "Now the eastern sky is turning a rose color!"

And so it was. The horizon turned a brilliant rose. Then golden rays appeared. Soon the sun itself rose into view. The villagers laughed and cried, knowing their long night was over at last.

Then out of the east, the golden phoenix appeared. It flew to Hui Niang and bowed its head in sorrow.

"My son is dead," Hui Niang told the villagers in a broken voice. "He died bringing back the sun."

Bao Chu's mother was torn with grief. But she was also proud that her son had completed his father's quest. Bao Chu would be a hero to his people forever.

To this day, the star of Liu Chun shines in the eastern sky just before dawn. Now it is called the Morning Star. And every day, the phoenix lifts the sun on its back. The wings of the phoenix turn the eastern sky purple, rose, and gold. And then the sun rises into the sky, warming the earth and all its people.

INSIGHTS

Bao Chu had quite some difficulty rescuing the sun. But at least he only had one sun to deal with.

The Chinese used to believe that ten suns existed. One by one the suns took turns shining down from the sky.

There came a day when all ten suns took it upon themselves to appear together. The intense heat threatened to burn up the earth.

The Chinese emperor decided he had to take action. So he sent a talented archer named Yi to shoot nine of the suns down. Yi did as he was ordered, and all was well again.

The idea of the ten suns continued to haunt the Chinese, however. It was believed that if more than one sun appeared at the same time, it meant the Chinese government was about to fall.

In China the phoenix was a special bird. It was said that buried treasure could be found close to wherever a phoenix perched.

One story tells of a farmer who spotted a phoenix and starting digging near it. Finding some funny-looking earth, he decided it must somehow be valuable. So he took it to the emperor.

But the emperor was not pleased. The strange-looking clump of earth had an unpleasant smell and didn't seem to have any use. He decided to send it away.

However, some of the stuff accidentally fell onto the emperor's food. When he took a bite, he found it was the best food he'd ever had. He ordered that the substance be sprinkled on all of his meals to enhance the flavor.

People all over the world flavor their food with this substance even today. Its name? Salt.

continued

Many cultures are known for worshipping several gods—gods of the water, sky, fire, etc. The Chinese went one step further and worshipped household gods. In fact, sometimes more gods than people inhabited a house.

For example, there was the Lord and Lady of the Bed in the bedroom and a god who guarded each door. There was even a god of the bathroom.

The most important of these household deities was the kitchen god. Once a year he would ascend to heaven and report to the Supreme Being on the actions of everyone in the house.

For this reason, people offered the kitchen god many sticky treats. They hoped to seal the lips of this nosy deity and keep him quiet.

Many Chinese believe in reincarnation (being reborn in another body after death). But some believe there is also a hell where most of the dead go first.

According to some people, there are 18 hells, each governed by a god called a "Yama-king." Each hell is reserved for the punishment of different crimes.

The Chinese also believe that those punishments always fit the crime. For example, murderers may be flung on top of sharp swords. Or those who speak against the gods might have their tongues ripped out.

After punishment, the soul is placed before a Yama-king. He decides what form the soul will take at rebirth.

A book called the Register of Life and Death is kept in hell. It shows when a person is ready to die. At the right time a person's soul is plucked from its body and sent to hell for the proper punishment.

However, sometimes the wrong soul is taken by accident. When the error is discovered, the soul is allowed to return to earth, reenter its body, and continue living. For this reason even today many Chinese keep the bodies of the dead for several days before burial.

Not everyone goes to hell when they die, according to the Chinese. Souls of the good go to live with the gods on the K'un-lun Mountain. Or they go to the "Land of Extreme Felicity in the West," which is the Chinese paradise. After spending some time in paradise, they may return to earth to be reborn as a king, queen, or other powerful person.

Many ancient Chinese myths are lost forever, thanks to a man named Li Szu. In 213 B.C., Li Szu proposed to the emperor that all books—except technical books—be burned.

The law remained in effect until 191 B.C. At that time scholars were allowed to start rewriting lost texts. But some writers felt they had a free hand when it came to rewriting old myths. For this reason many of the ancient stories we know of today are probably not the true originals.

GILGAMESH

VOCABULARY PREVIEW

Below is a list of words that appear in the story. Read the list and get to know the words before you start the story.

arrogant—boastful; conceited
defy—disobey; challenge
destined—certain; decided ahead of time
downcast—discouraged; sad
fickle—changeable; uncertain
grappled—wrestled; struggled
justly—fairly; with respect
menace—threat; danger
mock—make fun of; insult
mortal—human
nobles—upper-class people
recounting—retelling
sacred—valuable; important
scurrying—scrambling; moving quickly
spite—hatred; ill will
summit—top; peak
tyrant—dictator; harsh or cruel ruler
unleashed—released; set free
wan—pale; sickly
warily—with care

Main Characters

Anu—sky god; king of the gods
Aruru—goddess of creation; creator of earth and people
Enkidu—Gilgamesh's best friend

Gilgamesh—King of Uruk; son of goddess Ninsun
Humbaba—monster who guards the Cedar Mountain
Ishtar—goddess of love
Ninsun—minor goddess known for her wisdom; mother of
   Gilgamesh

GILGAMESH

A myth from Babylonia

*Gilgamesh is not only a king—he is part god.
But his people find it hard to put up with his
cruelty. So the gods send an unusual being to
teach Gilgamesh a few lessons.*

*G*ilgamesh[1] walked alone on the great wall of Uruk.[2] The wall's huge, rose-colored boulders reflected the bright afternoon sunlight. Within those walls stretched the city, with all its marketplaces, temples, palaces, and mud houses.

"A fine city," Gilgamesh said to himself. "The finest in all the world."

Gilgamesh was Uruk's king, and he was proud of the walls that he had built himself. Their tops were so wide and strong that warriors could drive great chariots on them. Uruk had withstood many attacks because of the strength of its walls and the fierceness of its king.

"My people should be grateful," Gilgamesh said to himself. "I keep them safe from our enemies."

However, his people were unhappy, and Gilgamesh knew it. The city leaders often brought complaints to the king's attention—complaints which made him angry.

"Why aren't my people happy?" he growled. "They have no right to tell me what to do. After all, I'm more than a king. I am a god!"

[1] (gil´ ga mesh)
[2] (ūr´ uk) Uruk was an ancient city between the Tigris and Euphrates rivers. The site is now part of Iraq.

But Gilgamesh knew that he was only part god. True, his mother was the goddess Ninsun.[3] But his father, although a king, had been **mortal.**

Even being only part god made Gilgamesh the most powerful and bravest of all mortals. No wrestler could defeat him, and he was the cleverest hunter of all.

Even so, Gilgamesh was **downcast.** He hated his mortal side. He knew he had to die someday, as surely as the lions he hunted.

"It isn't fair that I must die!" cried Gilgamesh, gazing over his city. He suddenly wanted to strike out, to break down the mighty walls with his fist. But what good would that do? Death awaited him, and he was helpless to do anything about it.

The people of Uruk could not guess Gilgamesh's thoughts as they watched him pace the walls. He looked like a proud and brave man, not someone who was worried about dying.

His body was muscled and he held his head high. His black curly hair and beard shone in the sun. His fierce dark eyes were large and shining. From afar, it was easy to admire him.

But when Gilgamesh came back down into his city, the citizens didn't stop to pay their respects. Shopkeepers and **nobles** alike hurried to get out of his path.

As always, the king tore through the city. He challenged a young man to a wrestling match. But the youth ducked out of sight without a word.

Gilgamesh finally raided a house, leaving with a bunch of dates. The king never even bothered to thank the occupants. He felt it was his right to take what he pleased. He was strong and he was king. And he didn't want his people to forget it.

When Gilgamesh returned to his palace, his people huddled together and whispered to each other. "This is our king! He's supposed to be wise as well as mighty. He's supposed to help and protect us, not lay waste to our homes!"

---

[3] (nin´ soon) Ninsun was a minor goddess whose temple was in Uruk.

"We must do something," one noble remarked.

"What can we do? Our king never listens to our pleas," answered another.

"Gilgamesh doesn't listen to *us*. But he might listen to someone of his own kind. We must ask the gods for help."

The nobles went to a temple to beg help from Aruru,[4] the goddess of creation.

"Please listen to our prayers, great Aruru," they called to her. "You created the earth and all its creatures. Only you can make a man who is Gilgamesh's equal. Create another mortal who can overcome our king's terrible pride, for we can stand no more of this **tyrant!"**

The goddess Aruru heard the nobles and left her place in the heavens. She soon appeared near the Euphrates—the great river which flowed by Uruk. The goddess wasn't sure at first how to answer the prayer. So she knelt down on the riverbank and thought long and hard. The wet, muddy clay seemed to give her an answer.

Aruru picked up a handful of clay and closed her eyes. Pictures filled her head—pictures of great heroes and gods. One in particular stood out from all the others—that of Anu,[5] father of all the gods.

"Yes," she whispered. "I will make a man who looks like Anu."

Aruru prayed to Anu as she pushed and pulled the clay, her eyes still closed tight. Before long she could feel the clay come to life in her hands. She lowered her creation to the ground and opened her eyes.

A living man lay sleeping on the ground in front of her. Aruru named him Enkidu.[6] Then she returned to her home among the gods.

This Enkidu was no ordinary creature. Although he was shaped like a god, he had a wild look about him. His body was covered with short, rough hair like a bull. His mind was untamed as well, filled with the memories and thoughts of

[4] (a roo´ roo)
[5] (a´ noo)
[6] (en kē´ du)

beasts. He knew nothing about human beings.

For many days after his creation, Enkidu lived in the wild among the animals. He ran with the gazelles,[7] easily keeping up with them. He grazed in the fields and joined herds of wild beasts at the watering hole. He was wild and free and happy.

Enkidu was smart too. He filled up pits dug by hunters to catch animals. And he helped beasts escape when they got caught in traps.

One young hunter grew angry and confused when, day after day, he found all his traps ruined. "Who can be doing this?" he asked himself.

So the hunter set a trap and hid behind a nearby tree. Then he waited to see who or what would come along and undo his work.

At last Enkidu arrived and destroyed the trap. But Enkidu's animal sense told him that something was wrong. He peeked behind the tree and discovered the hunter. Enkidu silently stared at the man.

The hunter was so frightened that he couldn't move. The wild, hairy creature seemed neither beast nor human.

"You're a monster!" gasped the hunter.

But Enkidu could not understand what the hunter said. He knew no human words. So without a sound, Enkidu turned and walked away into the desert.

The hunter picked up the animals he had trapped and hurried away. He knew that the king must be informed of this strange **menace** that was running free.

So the young hunter journeyed to Uruk. When he came before Gilgamesh, he described the monster he had seen.

But Gilgamesh had heard many stories of monsters invading his territory. He hardly listened to them any more. Still, he thought he had better do something—just in case the story was true. So Gilgamesh called a priestess to come to his throne room.

"There are reports of a strange creature in the desert," the king said to the priestess. "Perhaps he is a man, perhaps he is

---

[7] Gazelles are small antelopes that live in desert regions.

an animal. I want you to go and find out for yourself. If he is human, capture him and bring him here."

The priestess dressed in her finest silk robe and most glittering jewelry. And she put on her sweetest perfume.

The young hunter led the priestess to the watering hole and left her. As she waited, a gentle breeze carried her perfumed scent across the desert.

When evening fell, Enkidu and a herd of gazelles came to the watering hole. However, the gazelles smelled the woman and ran away. Enkidu smelled her, too, but did not run. He approached her **warily.** He had never come upon anything like this priestess.

"Come here, strange fellow!" said the priestess. Curiosity drew Enkidu closer.

"People told me you were a monster," she said, touching his hand. "But now I see they were wrong. You are a human being—a fine and godlike human being!"

Enkidu could not understand what the priestess said because he still knew no human words. But he was fascinated by the strange, sweet sounds the priestess made. He was struck, too, by her beauty—so unlike any animal he'd ever seen.

The priestess stayed with Enkidu for six days. During that time, he began to speak.

"What are these sounds I'm making?" he asked the priestess.

"Words," explained the priestess. "People use them to understand each other."

"These words make me sad," said Enkidu. "I didn't know what sadness was until I had a word for it."

Enkidu became sadder and sadder by the day. At last he reached a decision.

"It's time for me to rejoin my fellow beasts," he said to the priestess. "That's where I belong."

But when Enkidu approached a herd of gazelles, they ran away from him. And when he tried to chase after the animals, he discovered that he could no longer keep up with them.

In despair, Enkidu returned to the priestess. "What has

happened to me?" he asked her. "Why have I become so weak and slow?"

"It's true that you've lost some of your strength and speed," the priestess explained. "But you've gained new skills and knowledge. You are becoming more human.

"You see, Enkidu, you were never an animal," she went on. "You belong with people. You're too intelligent to run wild for the rest of your life."

"But what shall I do?" wondered Enkidu.

"Come back to the city of Uruk with me," the priestess urged. "Our king, Gilgamesh, has heard of you. He wants to meet you."

The priestess told Enkidu about the beautiful city of Uruk. She spoke of its marketplaces, temples, palaces, and houses. She promised that Enkidu would enjoy the company of other people just as he had once enjoyed the company of animals.

Then she told Enkidu about Gilgamesh the king—how strong and swift he was and also how cruel and selfish.

Enkidu was disturbed by the description. "Surely this Gilgamesh knows he must treat his fellow creatures with respect," he said. "The animals I roamed with are wild and don't know the gentler ways of humans. But at least they don't fight each other for amusement."

"I think Gilgamesh could learn a thing or two from you," the priestess remarked with a smile.

"Take me to Uruk," Enkidu demanded. "I want to meet this king."

So the priestess led Enkidu to the city of the mighty Gilgamesh. As they approached the gates, the people gathered around and admired the priestess' companion.

"He's the equal of the king," one said.

Another objected, saying, "No, he's not as tall."

"But he's stronger," the first one answered. "Look at the size of his arms and legs."

While news of Enkidu spread among the people, Gilgamesh lay sleeping in the palace. The king's slumber was suddenly interrupted by a nightmare.

Gilgamesh dreamed he saw a falling star rush earthward

from the sky. In his dream he rushed out of his palace and ran to the place where the star had fallen. He found a huge stone there, bright and glittering like a beautiful jewel.

The king knew that the stone was of great value, and he wanted to take it home. But try as he might, he couldn't move it—the strange stone seemed to fight against him.

This immovable object disturbed Gilgamesh. He had never encountered a man, beast, or thing he couldn't control.

At the end of his dream, the people of Uruk came from the city to gaze at the stone and worship it.

Gilgamesh awoke with a start. Filled with fear, he told his dream to his mother, the goddess Ninsun.

"Your dream means good news," she told her son. "True, you will meet a creature as strong as you, and the two of you will struggle. But this creature will become your friend. Much good will come of your friendship."

By the next evening, Gilgamesh had nearly forgotten about his dream. Gilgamesh and a group of his friends set out in the streets of Uruk. They intended to tear through the town as usual, doing as they pleased with the townspeople and their belongings.

But just when Gilgamesh was about to fling open the door of a private home and go inside, his way was blocked. Enkidu stood in the doorway, preventing the king from entering.

Gilgamesh stared at Enkidu in surprise. "How dare anyone block my way!" growled Gilgamesh.

With a mighty yell, the king threw himself at Enkidu. Gone was his memory of his dream and his mother's words. His only thought was the match at hand.

For what seemed like hours the two men **grappled.** Enkidu grunted as Gilgamesh slammed him into a wall. But Enkidu quickly gained his balance again. He rushed at Gilgamesh and threw him to the ground.

That still wasn't the end. Gilgamesh was on his feet in a flash, ready to continue.

And so it went. First one, then the other seemed close to triumph. But neither could claim victory.

The townspeople heard the noise and soon gathered

around. They stared in amazement at the two men. Never before had their leader been so evenly matched.

At long last Gilgamesh released his grip. He stood back and let out a hearty laugh. "I've never known any man with strength to match my own!" he cried.

"Nor have I ever met any beast as strong as you," answered Enkidu. "You are, indeed, a great warrior. But are you a great king?

"What do you mean?" Gilgamesh demanded.

"Can a king who hurts his people without a thought be called great?"

For once, Gilgamesh looked ashamed. "No," he answered quietly. Suddenly he remembered his dream and what his mother told him. He stared at Enkidu with growing awareness.

Without another word, Gilgamesh stepped up to Enkidu and embraced him. "I dreamed of you last night. We were **destined** to meet. You must come live in my palace," Gilgamesh insisted. "You will have the finest clothes, wine, food—everything you will ever need."

"I would be honored," Enkidu replied.

And that's how it began. Almost immediately the two became the best of friends. They were both delighted to have met their equals.

Enkidu also became a favorite of the people of Uruk, who knew he was the answer to their prayers.

"Enkidu is wise," the people said. "He will show Gilgamesh that it takes more than physical strength to be a good king."

Enkidu didn't disappoint them. Patiently and gently, he would say to Gilgamesh again and again, "The father of the gods has given you great power. But the gods intend for you to rule **justly,** not selfishly. Do good for your people. Do not misuse your power."

Gilgamesh learned Enkidu's lesson little by little. As time went by, he became a wise ruler. He was fair and kind to his people and no longer needed Enkidu's gentle reminders.

Finally the people of Uruk had no reason to fear their king. When Gilgamesh walked down the street, people didn't hurry away. They stayed to admire and praise their mighty ruler. They also honored Enkidu, the friend who was always at the king's side.

❖   ❖   ❖

One day Gilgamesh found his friend sitting alone in deep sadness. There were tears in Enkidu's eyes and a frown creased his brow.

"My friend, why do you sigh?" asked Gilgamesh. "Why do you look so bitter?"

"I've grown weary and can no longer run swiftly," Enkidu replied. "This easy life has made me forget who I really am."

"What do you mean?" Gilgamesh said with a laugh. "You're stronger and swifter than any man in the city—except perhaps for me."

"You don't know what it's like to be far from home," said Enkidu, raising his voice. "You've always lived in this fine palace. But part of me is still an animal, still untamed. That part of me belongs to the wilderness. Oh, how I long to be free and wild again!"

But they both knew that Enkidu could not go back. He could no longer run fast enough to keep up with the wild beasts. Even if he could, he would no longer be accepted among them. Enkidu would be alone if he returned to the wilderness. And so would Gilgamesh.

Gilgamesh thought the matter over for a while. Then he said to Enkidu, "I suppose we'll both soon grow old and weak, living in all this luxury. Warriors like us need battles to fight, challenges to meet."

"Yes," groaned Enkidu, "but what challenges are left for us?"

"Well," began Gilgamesh, "there is something I've been wanting to do for quite a while. And this just might be the time to do it—with you at my side."

"And what might that be?" asked Enkidu with a spark of interest in his eye.

"I'm not just talking about an adventure. If we do this successfully, we would make life better for everyone in

Uruk."

"What is it? Tell me!" exclaimed Enkidu. He was definitely interested now.

"Have you heard of the Cedar Forest?"

"Yes. I learned of that place when I lived with the animals."

"Can you imagine being able to use wood from such a forest?"

Enkidu frowned. "Think what you're saying," he said. "Don't you realize that the monster Humbaba[8] guards that forest? Enlil, the god of storms, put him in charge there ages ago."

"So," said Gilgamesh with a smile, "I think you see our challenge. If we kill Humbaba, we'll be free to cut down the cedar trees. In the place of mud, our people will have fragrant wood to build their houses with."

"A challenge is one thing," replied Enkidu. "But to openly **defy** the gods is another."

"And do you plan to spend your life quietly obeying the gods, Enkidu? What sort of punishment do you fear from them? Death? Wake up, my friend. We'll all die sooner or later. The gods live forever. We cannot."

"But Gilgamesh, Humbaba spits fire and roars like thunder. He can hear an enemy approaching from miles away. And his magic brings weakness upon anyone who tries to enter. This is no challenge. This is madness!"

Gilgamesh glared at his friend. Traces of his hot temper showed. "Well, then, I guess I'll just have to fight the mighty Humbaba by myself."

Enkidu studied his friend. Then he sighed. "You'll do no such thing. If you're determined to take up this quest, I'll go with you. Friends don't turn their backs on friends. But don't get the idea that I approve of this craziness of yours."

The people of Uruk didn't approve either. They were angry, afraid, and certain they would lose both of their heroes. They begged Gilgamesh and Enkidu not to go. But the two

---

[8] (hoom ba´ ba)

warriors would not listen to their pleas.

"We're doing this for you," Gilgamesh told the citizens. "Please don't worry. We'll soon be back safe and sound—and with plenty of wood!"

To comfort his people, Gilgamesh prayed to the gods. "Oh, mighty ones!" he shouted to the sky. "I know the Cedar Forest belongs to you. Yet Humbaba, the watchman of the forest, is evil. He prevents my people from having wood for their houses.

"I don't wish to make you angry by killing something that belongs to you," the king continued. "I am merely thinking of the good of my people. For this reason, I'm asking your help in ridding the earth of this evil named Humbaba."

When their supplies were ready, Gilgamesh and Enkidu armed themselves and departed through the city gates.

"I will lead the way," said Enkidu. "I know the wilderness with its hidden trails. My friends the animals also told me where Humbaba lives."

So Enkidu led Gilgamesh across the plains, along the very paths he had roamed when he ran with the wild herds.

As Gilgamesh had hoped, Enkidu seemed more and more renewed by the coming adventure. As the men walked and hunted along the way, Enkidu's strength returned. Although he could no longer run as fast as the gazelle, he regained much of his old swiftness.

The two companions walked for many days. They drank at water holes which were full of fresh water. Hawks and eagles circled in the sunlight.

At last they stopped and Enkidu pointed ahead. Before them stood a mountain covered with tall cedar trees.

"The Cedar Forest, **sacred** to the gods," whispered Enkidu. "This is where the terrible Humbaba lives. We'll have to be more careful now—and quiet, too. Humbaba may even be listening to us this minute."

The two warriors crept silently up the mountain, hiding behind trees and bushes. About halfway up the mountain, they found themselves standing before a towering gate built of timber and stone.

"At last!" exclaimed Gilgamesh. "The gate to Humbaba's home!"

But as Enkidu opened the gate, weakness overcame him and he fell to the ground. While Gilgamesh stopped to help his friend, the two could hear Humbaba **scurrying** away to the top of the mountain.

"We'll never defeat that monster now," Enkidu moaned. "His magic has weakened me. I can hardly move."

"And what would you have us do—turn back?" asked Gilgamesh. "I swear never to return to Uruk until this monster is dead—or I am. Come, Enkidu. We must stand by each other. Stay close to me. I'm sure your weakness will pass."

So Gilgamesh helped his friend continue up Cedar Mountain. They were amazed by the height and beauty of the trees rising above them. They enjoyed the shade and the cedar scent filling the air. But they knew the monster Humbaba waited for them at the **summit.**

When nightfall came, it was Gilgamesh who was overcome with weakness and fell into a deep sleep. A terrible dream came to him—a dream in which the earth crumbled and fire rained from the sky. Gilgamesh saw the mountain top burning. From out of the surrounding smoke, he heard a voice cry out.

"Gilgamesh! Gilgamesh!"

Gilgamesh opened his eyes. Enkidu was shaking him, saying his name over and over. "Gilgamesh! You're awake at last! Your sleep was so deep and long, I almost mistook it for death."

"I've had an awful dream," said Gilgamesh, rubbing his eyes. He described it to Enkidu.

"But this is good, Gilgamesh!" exclaimed Enkidu. "Your dream surely means victory for us—and death for Humbaba!"

The warriors made a sacrifice to the gods and continued up Cedar Mountain. At last, they came to Humbaba's magic grove[9] of seven cedar trees. The winds began to blow, and

---

[9] A grove is a cluster of trees. Many cultures and peoples believed that groves were magical.

thunder and lightning filled the sky.

"Are the gods against us, even after my prayers?" Gilgamesh wondered.

Suddenly Humbaba stepped out from among the magic cedars. He was truly a terrible sight, as tall as the cedars he guarded and as wild as the storm swirling around him.

"You are trespassing in the sacred forest of the gods!" Humbaba bellowed in a voice louder than the thunder. His great eyes glared down at them. "Leave at once—while you still can!"

Any mortal would have turned and fled at these words. But Gilgamesh was no mere mortal. Bravely, he took his sword and his ax and stepped forward to do battle.

"Humbaba, I have sworn not to leave until I have completed my mission," he said. "My people need wood. And if that means I have to kill you for it, then so be it."

"I'm afraid you're mistaken," said the monster with a wicked grin. "It is not I who will die. You are the one who should fear for your life!"

And with that, the mighty Humbaba rushed toward Gilgamesh. But Gilgamesh was ready for him. The king quickly sidestepped his opponent's rush and Humbaba stumbled into a tree.

Roaring with anger, the monster straightened and turned back toward Gilgamesh. Then with a huge sweep of his arm, Humbaba knocked the king off his feet. But Gilgamesh jumped up, ready to continue.

The storm raged while the two struggled. The trees bent under a mighty wind. Suddenly the wind and rain turned against the monster. Lightning blazed, setting the mountain top on fire.

"The gods have heard our prayers," thought Enkidu.

Finally Gilgamesh struck Humbaba a mighty blow with his ax. The monster fell senseless to the ground. The storm still swirled around them.

"Is he dead?" Enkidu asked.

Before Gilgamesh could answer, Humbaba moved his head and opened his eyes. He tried to rise, but his power was gone.

"Gilgamesh," the monster begged, "let me live and I will serve you. I'll help you with my magic."

Gilgamesh felt pity for the fallen Humbaba. "Shall I let him go?" he asked Enkidu.

But Enkidu didn't trust the monster. "He's clever and dangerous, Gilgamesh. He'll turn on you. You must kill him."

"Silence, Enkidu!" snapped Humbaba. "Who are *you,* anyway? A palace servant, nothing more! How dare you tell your king what to do!"

"See how his evil magic works," Enkidu said. "He'd turn you against me."

The king knew Enkidu's words were true. So he drew his sword and struck the monster. Then Enkidu picked up his own sword and struck yet another blow. Gilgamesh let fall one final blow, and Humbaba was dead.

With the death of Humbaba, the storm calmed. Everything around them was burned and lifeless. Gilgamesh's dream had come true.

Enkidu looked around. Down the mountain slopes he could see huge trees moving gently in the breeze. Small green stems quickly popped out of the burned and blackened soil. All evil had vanished from the Cedar Mountain.

"We've won the giant's forest!" exclaimed Gilgamesh in delight. "All these fine trees are ours. Now our people can use wood instead of mud to build their houses."

The two companions rested a bit and then made their long journey back to Uruk.

At the city gates, a crowd of people joyfully rushed forward to greet Gilgamesh and Enkidu. How grateful everyone was to have their king and his mighty companion home again! And now the two were greater heroes than ever. Feasts and celebrations went on into the night.

❖   ❖   ❖

But even as the people rejoiced, trouble was brewing. Ishtar,[10] the goddess of love, caught sight of the celebrations from afar.

[10] (ish´ tar)

She was overwhelmed by Gilgamesh's beauty and could think of nothing else.

As gods and goddesses often did, Ishtar decided that she wanted the handsome mortal for herself. So when the feasting ended, she met Gilgamesh alone in the street.

"Come with me and be my husband, Gilgamesh," she said. "I am powerful and can give you many things. Listen, I'll give you a golden chariot set with jewels. And I'll tame the demons of the storm to pull it for you. People everywhere will bow down to you."

Gilgamesh said nothing and tried to pass her by. He knew this **fickle** goddess was dangerous. But Ishtar blocked his way and drew closer. She was very beautiful and her magic was strong.

"The sweet smell of cedar will fill our house," she continued. "We'll be happy together. Remember that you are part god. Do you deserve less than a goddess for a wife?"

Gilgamesh drew back from her. "Why should I marry you, Ishtar?" he replied. "Your past lovers haven't been very lucky. You loved none of them for long. Shall I list them?"

Ishtar frowned, but Gilgamesh went on. "A great bird once loved you. You thanked him for his love by breaking his wings.

"A handsome shepherd loved you too," continued Gilgamesh. "You turned him into a wolf when you tired of him. His own hounds and shepherd boys drove him from his home and flocks.

"And what about that gardener you turned into a mole?" he added. "I'm sure there were others. Would you care to complete the list, Ishtar?"

"If I was unkind to others," insisted Ishtar, "it was because I had not yet met my one true love. You are the one I love, Gilgamesh. I could never do wrong to you."

But the king was too wise to believe her words. "I would end up as they did, Ishtar," he answered the goddess. "I will never be your husband."

Ishtar bitterly stormed away. Gilgamesh hoped that would be an end to the matter. But he knew that Ishtar had a terrible temper. There was really no telling what she would do.

Gilgamesh was right to be concerned. Ishtar went directly to her father, Anu—the king of all the gods.

"Father," the furious goddess cried, "Gilgamesh has insulted me! He has accused me of doing terrible things. Worst of all, he has refused to be my husband!"

Anu looked at his daughter thoughtfully. "You aren't known for your kindness to your lovers," he said. "Perhaps Gilgamesh only told the truth."

Ishtar wept great tears. "But Gilgamesh is different from the others!" she pleaded. "I love him! And he paid me back with **spite!**"

"And what would you have me do about it, daughter?"

"Give me the Bull of Heaven," she said. "I will turn it against this **arrogant** Gilgamesh."

"No, Ishtar, you can't let the Bull of Heaven loose in Uruk," replied Anu with shock in his voice. "He would kill all the people!"

"Father," said Ishtar, "if you don't grant my wish, I'll throw open the gates of the Underworld. All the dead will escape into the world of the living. Imagine the destruction *that* would cause!"

In the face of this terrible threat, Anu was forced to give in. He handed over the Bull of Heaven to Ishtar to use as she wished.

Ishtar quickly **unleashed** the bull within Uruk's walls. At once the bull began charging through the city, destroying everything in his path. Each time the great beast snorted, he killed a hundred people. He trampled Uruk's citizens under his mighty hooves. And when the bull flung his head and stamped his foot, buildings shook and toppled.

It looked as though the entire city would be destroyed. But as the bull approached the palace, Enkidu and Gilgamesh were there to face him.

The bull glared at the two heroes. Then with a roar, he charged straight at Enkidu.

Enkidu dodged the charge and seized the bull by its horns. The beast's hot breath burned Enkidu's face, and the hero had to release him. The bull slashed Enkidu with his tail, knocking the warrior to the ground.

But Enkidu caught hold of the monster's tail. His grip was firm and could not be shaken. Enkidu held the bull tight.

Then Gilgamesh quickly drew his sword and plunged it into the bull's neck.

The beast flung himself about for several minutes. Then giving one last snort, he dropped to the ground and died.

"Well, that's the end of that!" exclaimed Gilgamesh triumphantly. "Even the gods can't defeat me."

The goddess Ishtar heard Gilgamesh's boast. Standing above the celebrating people, she shouted, "Beware, Gilgamesh! You have insulted me for the last time!"

Even angrier than before, the goddess fled into the darkness.

The celebrations in Uruk went on late into the night. Gilgamesh took the giant horns of the Bull of Heaven and hung them on the palace wall.

But Enkidu was worried. Indeed, he had been uneasy ever since they had killed Humbaba. Would the gods punish them for killing their prize bull?

That night Enkidu had a nightmare. All the great gods met together and he listened as they talked.

"We have given these mortals everything they could possibly want!" murmured some. "We even created Enkidu to be Gilgamesh's friend," said others.

"These two defiant mortals have gone too far," said others. "The death of Humbaba was bad enough. But killing the Bull of Heaven is unforgivable. One of them must die!"

Enkidu awoke, troubled by his dream and feeling very ill. By evening he could not rise from his bed.

"I am dying," he weakly told Gilgamesh. "I knew it was unwise to **mock** the gods. Now they are taking their revenge."

"Nonsense," replied Gilgamesh. "Don't worry. You'll soon be up and about again."

But as Gilgamesh looked at his friend's **wan** face, he grew more and more worried.

"Is Enkidu right?" wondered Gilgamesh. "Are the gods

really going to punish me by taking away my best friend?"

As Enkidu lay in his bed, Gilgamesh never left his side. The king was panicked by the thought of losing Enkidu. But he tried not to let his friend see his worry. Instead, he cheered Enkidu by **recounting** tales of their adventures together.

"How we fought the first time we met!" said Gilgamesh, laughing.

"You were unmovable, like a rock!" replied Enkidu weakly.

"No more immovable than you."

They spoke of the many good days they had spent together. They remembered their long journey to the Cedar Mountain, their fight with Humbaba, and their victorious return. They also spoke of their triumph over the Bull of Heaven.

But Enkidu grew weaker. At last, with a final gasp, he closed his eyes and was silent.

Gilgamesh could find no heartbeat, no breath. He went wild with grief and roared and paced like a wild beast.

"It isn't fair!" he yelled. "It isn't fair that he should die when I was the one who angered the gods!"

But finally Gilgamesh grew quiet. He knew there was nothing he could do to bring his friend back to life. So he shut himself in his palace and grieved alone.

Gilgamesh wasn't the only one filled with sorrow. Everyone in Uruk mourned the passing of Enkidu, the kind hero who had once lived with the animals.

❖   ❖   ❖

Gilgamesh reigned as king for many more years. He had other adventures too—more than anyone can tell.

Yet the death of his dear friend scarred Gilgamesh. It made him still more bitter that all human life must end. So he searched for the key to everlasting life. But his search was in vain.

Still, Gilgamesh remained a good king. Whenever his old selfishness began to show itself, he would hear his departed friend Enkidu whisper, "The father of the gods has given you great power. But the gods intend for you to rule justly, not selfishly. Do good for your people. Do not abuse your power."

Even in death, Enkidu never really left Gilgamesh's side.

INSIGHTS

*G*ilgamesh has its roots in the ancient Sumerian civilization of southern Iraq. The epic myth is the earliest major recorded work of literature. And like many such early works, it serves as a record of religious traditions and beliefs.

The Sumerians recorded *Gilgamesh* on clay tablets. They used written symbols called *cuneiform*. In this type of writing, letters were formed by pressing a wedge-shaped stick into soft clay. *Cuneiform* comes from the Latin word *cuneus*, meaning "wedge."

The clay tablets used could be as large as great blocks or as small as bricks. Small tablets, about three by four inches, were used for mailing letters. The letters were even sent in clay envelopes!

It might seem that storage of these tablets could be a problem. But a later civilization maintained a huge library of about 22,000 clay tablets.

The Sumerian civilization is long gone. But the culture lives on through its writing and outstanding achievements.

For instance, the Sumerians were one of the first known people to use the wheel. And the Sumerian calendar system was so sophisticated that even today it astounds scholars. The 365-day year was one of the Sumerian concepts. (Though there were only 360 days in the regular Sumerian year, a five-day festival was added at the end.)

The Sumerians also came up with the 60-second minute and the 60-minute hour.

In 2000 B.C. the Sumerians were conquered by the Babylonians. This great empire absorbed the entire Sumerian culture, including its history and literature. So Gilgamesh became a Babylonian hero, and the tales about him began to include Babylonian gods and goddesses.

The real Gilgamesh was probably a king of Uruk—a Sumerian city near the Euphrates River. It is said that he ruled sometime between 2700 and 2500 B.C. As time passed, the deeds of this admired king grew legendary. Finally he became more a mythical figure than a real one.

Many of the events in the epic of *Gilgamesh* were apparently based on fact. For example, it's almost certain that the real king did travel to the wilderness to gather some much-needed wood for his people. But he probably didn't slay a monster named Humbaba. Most likely, Gilgamesh had to fight hostile forest tribes before being able to haul away the wood.

The version of the myth in this book ends with Enkidu's death. But as is hinted in the story, there's more to the Babylonian myth.

When Enkidu died, Gilgamesh grew determined to find the secret of everlasting life. So he sought out Utanapishtim, one of his ancestors who had been given everlasting life. Gilgamesh convinced Utanapishtim to reveal the location of the flower of youth.

But Gilgamesh was doomed to disappointment. On the way back to his kingdom, he became careless with the flower. As a result, a serpent ate it.

So instead of bringing everlasting youth to himself and his people, Gilgamesh gave it to snakes instead. This myth helped explain why snakes shed their skins and supposedly begin a new life each spring.

In another version of the Gilgamesh myth, the king calls upon Enkidu's spirit to learn about life after death. But Enkidu doesn't bring good news. He reports of a cheerless existence—especially for those whose bodies weren't properly buried.

To reach the Underworld, a dead person had to travel through seven dark regions. Once there, he or she was to remain enclosed forever in the "dwelling place of the shadows" with nothing to eat but mud. This was held to be the

fate of every person, good or evil. It's little wonder that
Gilgamesh wanted no part of it!